I0764370

Jewish and Indian and Other Stories

Jewish and Indian and Other Stories

H. C. KIM

The Hermit Kingdom Press
Cheltenham Seoul Bangalore Cebu

JEWISH AND INDIAN AND OTHER STORIES

For information address:

The Hermit Kingdom Press
Suite 407
3741 Walnut Street
Philadelphia, PA 19012
USA

http://www.TheHermitKingdomPress.com

ISBN 0-9723864-7-5

For my goddaughter Amanda

The firstborn of my best friend Ed Moseng

May she always live under justice and peace

Preface

I have spent many years living in Israel, thinking about the situation in that part of the world. I have spent many hours investigating Jewish history and texts, in an effort to understand and to contribute to a better understanding of Jewish experiences. I am glad that I am able to share my labor of love in the form of short stories. I hope that the stories will help in terms of better understanding and constructive thinking.

H. C. Kim
Jesus College
Cambridge
21 June 2004
22nd Birthday of Prince William of Wales

"We do not seek an agreement with the Arabs in order to secure the peace. Of course we regard peace as an essential thing. It is impossible to build up the country in a state of permanent warfare. But peace for us is a mean, and not an end. The end is the fulfillment of Zionism in its maximum scope. Only for this reason do we need peace, and do we need an agreement."

David Ben-Gurion
The First Prime Minister of the State of Israel

CONTENTS

Ibrahim

I felt uncomfortable every time he opened the door. I don't know why I let him bother me the way he did. After all, what I was doing was what I wanted to do. He had no right to be judge over me. But still, his eyes seemed to glare down at me whenever the opened door revealed my presence.

"Hi," I said, trying to sound confident.

"Welcome in," John said with an innocent cultic smile on his face.

"Thanks," I replied, losing my resolve.

"For what?" John said as if he had done no favors.

"For opening the door," I responded without thinking. John looked at me and smiled. I thought I detected a trace of sadness on his face.

"Hi, there, Jenn," Ibrahim said with a big smile. He seemed excited to see me as if he had just won a big bet. Come to think about it, that's how he always was when he greeted me.

"Hi, Ibrahim," I said, walking towards him.

I turned around to say something to John. But I only caught a glimpse of him closing the door behind him. The door shut behind him and he was alone in his room.

I quickly turned around. I don't know why but I felt the need to go into Ibrahim's room as soon as possible. The hallway was way too narrow for comfort. It seemed like it would cave in any moment. As small as the open space was in the common area, it would get smaller still. I was sure of it. The walls appeared unfriendly, like the walls of a dragon's stomach after a sacrifice is consumed.

"Wow, you are happy to see me!" Ibrahim said, smiling but oblivious.

It had become a daily ritual ever since Ibrahim moved in to live with John. John was from America with no ties to this country. He was here for one year and interested in maximizing his own experiences. He had no time to fuss over me or Ibrahim or our relationship.

It was different when Ibrahim lived with native people in a dormitory just a month before. The walls had eyes and ears. Even when I saw nothing and no one was around me, it was clear that people knew what I did – what we did.

To be honest, I was not afraid that words would travel back to my parents. Of course, if my father found out what I did with Ibrahim, I can't even begin to imagine what he would do. He would probably self-destruct. I was more afraid for his well-being than how he would act towards me. As strong as he was, I was his little girl. To him, I would always be that little girl who sat on his lap as he told stories of proud Arabs of the past.

Mom was different. She would disapprove, of course, educated by Catholic nuns her whole life. And she did make the life-view of the nuns her own. To her the body was the temple of Jesus Christ. The door was open only to the one admitted through the bond of holy matrimony. There was only one key. No copies were made.

But with mom, there was an acceptance of reality. She knew what the world was like, with all the pitfalls and sorrows. Her religious sensibilities did not immobilize her. The cozy Catholic world she built for herself in a village in northern Israel was no bubble. She read voraciously as a modern Arab woman. She knew what was out there without having spotted herself with the iniquities of the weak world.

I did not fear for her because she was a realist. She knew and accepted what came her way. Dad was the opposite. He was strong, but an idealist. And there lay his fundamental weakness. Well, at least when it came to me, his Achilles' heel.

"I want to hear all about your day," Ibrahim said in a gentle voice.

I looked at him and was impressed again by the sincerity in his eyes. There was something fundamentally attractive about Arab men. They were all good-natured, every single one that I met. Even the ones who tried to impress me by saying that they were terrorists for the Hizbollah were gentle souls with broad smiles. Perhaps, they were terrorists. Perhaps, they were liars. What did I care? I am a woman. How a man treats me on a personal level is all that I care about. Who cares what he does to others?

You may call me selfish, but I can guarantee you that this is how women generally feel. How else would you explain the stories of women in love with prisoners and so-called criminals? If he is good to a woman, that is good enough for her.

I did, of course, proclaim to mom and others that I wanted a good man. Who's going to say that they want a bad man? But secretly, I think most women long for men who are bad – or rather, those generally perceived to be bad by everyone. But the key is that this bad man would be good to her.

In fact, isn't love worth more when a perceived evil man can be good to one special person? It is a way of affirming her value. She is worth being good to even if the whole world should be cast into Hell.

In Ibrahim, I did not find an evil man. He was a decent man, a good man. In fact, I did not know too many evil Arab men. They were all polite and gentle. Even those convicted of terrorism by the Israeli police were gentle. I was convinced Arab men just got a bad rap.

That's probably how it was with Irish men. Irish guys were perceived as terrorists. The English probably treated the Irish like the scum of the world, like vermin who had to be wiped out. But I bet many members of the IRA were devout husbands and loving fathers. They were just like the Arab men that I know, I bet. They just got a bad rap.

"Ibrahim, you are so good to me," I testified. I recounted to him all the things that I did, and he listened attentively. Occasionally, he politely asked questions and sought elaboration in the details.

I felt loved. I felt treasured.

Without saying he loved me, Ibrahim showed me what a man in love is like. I completely trusted him.

"Ibrahim, here I am blabbering away about myself. Tell me about your day," I said, wanting to hold him.

"I was thinking about you," Ibrahim said, looking deeply into my eyes. I felt weak at the knees, and I was sitting down.

Every visit to Ibrahim was a source of joy to me because I felt like a treasured human being. He did not want to get physical right away, although from experience – many experiences – I knew that his passions ran deep. He proved beyond doubt that he desired me with his body and his all. But with every visit, Ibrahim showed self-control, a disciplined restraint that would put fire into my very being. Ibrahim was the first lover I had, so I assumed that all Arab men were like him. But I did not want to find out. I just wanted Ibrahim.

I knew that Jewish men were not like Ibrahim. I observed Israeli men at the cafeteria, and the brazen way they behaved towards each other and with Israeli women. They were conceited and lacked politeness.

I wondered if this behavior was due to their mandatory service in the army. Israeli Defense Forces are among the best in the world. I have heard them brag. As much as I hate to admit it, I don't doubt it. To maintain such a mean fighting machine, the soldiers are probably put through a program of dehumanization and desensitization. Their behavior certainly indicated such an attitude.

I am one of the few Arab women at the university, so I feel self-conscious. But I was convinced that the problem was not with me but with them. There was a kind of Israeli pride that forced them to look down on Arabs. I was not a woman to them. They never looked at me as a sexual being. To them, I was an Arab, the part of the collective Arabness, which they were taught to hate in the army and in their society.

They would look at me. And I saw contempt in their eyes, sometimes hatred, but never desire or respect. It was different with Arab men. They looked at me with gentleness. They perceived me as a woman with sexual powers. I even detected passionate lust in some of their stares. It made me feel valuable and wanted. I think it's fundamentally a need that women have. Although I can't speak for all women, I don't think that I am wrong. There is the need to be desired.

To me, Arab men are good because they treat me like a woman, like a human being. Both are inseparable. Israeli men are bad because they perceive me as an object, as a part of the Arab Other. It didn't matter to me that Arab men blew up buses and killed Israeli men. They deserved it for dehumanizing us Arab women, I will say in my anger. Certainly, it does not matter to me how good Israeli men are by an ethical standard, if they take away from me my rights as a woman. They are evil in my eyes.

Ibrahim and I talked for a long while. During the conversation, Ibrahim produced some fruit and cookies. He made sure that I was not thirsty or hungry. With what he had, he gave me his all. I knew he loved me. That is why I gave him what was most precious to me. And I had no regrets.

I slipped out early in the morning. I did not want to disturb John in the morning. As innocent as he looked, I knew that he knew what we were doing. I felt embarrassed about facing him in the morning. Maybe it was my Catholic upbringing. I remember Father Murphy from Ireland who used to tell us to keep pure like Holy Mary the Mother of God until we were properly married in the house of God. Maybe it was the earnest entreaty of Father Murphy that imbued me with a sense of guilt.

John is a Christian. He actually organized a Christian Union group at the Hebrew University of Jerusalem. There were about five people meeting every week from what I understand. All of them were from America. John had invited me a few times after I told him that I was Catholic. "You are a Christian sister!" he would say excitedly. John kind of reminded me of Father Murphy, although John was a mixture of German and Italian. They both had the same gentle aura that smacked of perfect inner peace.

I often wondered what John was doing here in Israel. There must be a thousand other places that he could go to, which were more interesting. Germany, for instance, with its fairytale stories probably held considerable charm. China with its glorious and long history probably captivates beyond words, I bet.

Israel was basically a series of concrete buildings made hurriedly to accommodate large wave of immigrations from Europe and Russia. There was nothing architecturally beautiful in most neighborhoods. Russian friends of mine used to say that buildings here looked worse than the big communist living blocks behind the Iron Curtain. People with Israel's ancient history often seemed to lose their dream-based admiration upon arrival. Why did John come?

The day flew by relatively quickly and the much awaited evening came. It was Friday, and John was to visit some friends in Haifa. Ibrahim and I had the apartment to ourselves, so we went all out. Ibrahim did shopping for food that we were going to cook. As always, Ibrahim's excited smile greeted me.

"Guess what?" Ibrahim said enthusiastically.

"What?" I said, my eyes becoming wider and wider.

"I bought a new machine!" Ibrahim exclaimed.

"Oh!" I tried to sound excited. But I had to admit that a new machine did not capture my interest as it did his. It must be a guy thing.

"It's a George Foreman barbecue," Ibrahim continued like he discovered gold.

"You are really cute, like a child," I teased him. Ibrahim looked a bit hurt by this, so I added, "But you are tough, tougher than all the Israelis in the university."

Ibrahim seemed pleased by my conclusive comment.

"Guess what we can do with this machine?" Ibrahim asked.

"What?" I responded with a question, while marveling at his unceasing enthusiasm.

"We are going to barbecue chicken breasts in olive oil and cumin," Ibrahim explained. "And guess what we are going to call it?"

"What?" I said, humoring him.

"Jenny's Heaven," Ibrahim answered.

"That is really sweet, Ibrahim," I said with tears welling up. He seemed to think about me all the time, and I liked it. It moved my being.

Ibrahim cooked, apparently stealing glances at a piece of paper. He probably got the recipe from his mother. He was a certified mama's boy. No two ways about it. But I thought it was really sweet that he tried to impress me by hiding the recipe. We had been dating for two years and it still felt like he was courting me. I smiled and looked at him.

Soon, the meal was prepared. Ibrahim opened a bottle of kosher wine he bought at the local grocery store. Everything there was kosher, even the sugar. We were living in the Jewish state after all. But as Arabs, we created our little haven in this place. Ibrahim always made the special effort, and that made the meal that much more special. I sat there and thought about how lucky we were to have each other. I believed that we would spend the rest of our lives together and that we would be happy.

The evening quickly passed by in our togetherness. We talked and we laughed like there was no tomorrow. We forgot what was going on outside. All the tragedy and sadness that affected the Arabic people seemed to fade into the background. I had always told my parents that I would move to Australia where my dad's brother lived and live there. I hated being here in Israel and being dehumanized by Jews. But with Ibrahim by my side, I did not care any more.

I did not care that the Israelis looked at me as if something had crawled out of a big, ugly rock on the Mount of Olives. I did not care that my rights were legally restricted by pro-Jewish, anti-Arabic Israeli laws. I did not care that the taxes paid to the Jewish state by Arabs were not used to provide the same kind of services for Arabs who were Israeli citizens. I only cared that I was with Ibrahim. Together, we could overcome any obstacles. Together, we would make Israel our home.

I woke up early in the morning as if my body had a permanent alarm clock. Then, I realized that John was not there. Once woken up, I could not go back to sleep. I looked at Ibrahim, and was surprised that he looked forlorn in his sleep. I thought I detected wrinkle lines on his forehead and wondered what a man of 22 had to worry about. I looked at his lips and they seemed to be pressing against each other like he was gritting his teeth in pain. I looked at his eyes and thought I saw sadness behind those closed eyelids.

I was disappointed. I felt sad because his vulnerable appearance belied his true state. I did not fulfill his every need. Even while lying in my arms, he looked like he was worrying and not at peace. I saw weakness in his visage that I had never imaged existed. I felt a motherly instinct towards him for the first time as I beheld the helpless boy before me.

But the other side of me was disgusted. I was turned off by his evident weakness. There he lay, like the Arab portrayed by Jews, as demoralized and cowardly. He was the reason why Arabs were still oppressed by Jews in Israel. His weakness and the weaknesses of men like him deprived me of my freedom and my parents of their human dignity. Ibrahim was a part of the problem.

It was then, for the first time, I felt disgust towards him. I had never imagined that I could feel this way about Ibrahim, my knight in shining armor. Before me stood not a brave knight but a lowly peasant who could not defend the honor of that which was most precious to him. I doubted for the first time if he was the one. For the first time, I felt insecure in his presence. I did not like the feeling one bit. I felt like running. I felt like dashing at a top speed towards Jaffa Gate, without stopping. Then, run through the Old City towards

Jericho. The vast Judean Desert would offer more comfort at the moment.

I did not feel like sleeping any more. I wrote a little note, lying to Ibrahim that I had to work that day and that I did not want to spoil the evening by telling him in advance about it the evening before. I felt exonerated in my lie as I felt he had lied to me with promises of security and safety. I didn't care about material or financial safety, but I did care about my peace of mind. I felt that this day, that evaporated. Ibrahim lay there, helpless and as a liar.

I closed the door behind me, still in the darkness of the early morn. I could not stop the tears from flowing. I cried and I sobbed all the way back home. I wanted to break the morning calm like my calm was broken. I did not restrain myself, but I received no sympathy. All were asleep, even the birds.

I made excuses for the next few days and did not visit Ibrahim. As it was exam period, this must have appeared natural to Ibrahim. He did not protest. I must confess that I wish he had. I wish that he had forced me to come and be with him. I did not want him to be a gentleman. But he was. This only confirmed in my mind that he was helpless. He could not protect me. He was not my knight in shining armor.

I confided in my best friend. I did not want to, but I could not help myself. I made her swear secrecy, but I knew that her memory of her solemn oath would be as short-lived as her desire to spread the news intense, like a quickly burning tree in a desert. But I longed to share, and I could not restrain myself.

As soon as I unloaded my heart, I felt better. But soon, fear set in. What if she tells someone? What if Ibrahim finds out? Would he love me less? And I tried to convince myself that I did not love him less, although I knew that I did. I did not want Ibrahim to love me less. Despite what was happening to me, I wanted to have Ibrahim's desire and his undivided devotion.

Was I being selfish? I don't know. I did not care. I wanted his love until I figured out what I really wanted. I felt as if this were a matter of self-survival, my self-preservation. This was my ethic, which superceded any ethics that dead philosophers had sprouted. After all, what did they know about me? Only I know myself. And I wanted both. To have the luxury to decide whether Ibrahim was the one, while he was bound to me in eternal allegiance of love.

One day, I walked into the small garden area enclosed within the main building. The sunshine was refreshing and gave me the warmth that I needed. As I lost myself in a reverie, I realized a presence near me. I opened my eyes and beheld a human form. There was the bright Mediterranean sun behind the undecipherable face. His head seemed to glow like the head of Moses descending from Mount Sinai with stone tablets of the Law. Father Murphy was vivid in his description of the awesome presence of God and its reflection in the person of Moses.

"Hi, Jenny," a familiar voice said.

"Hi, John," I replied. It was good to see him again.

"May I sit down?" John said like the Southern Baptist gentleman that he was.

"Sure thing," I replied.

"We haven't seen you around lately," John said and then quickly added, "Ibrahim misses you."

"Oh?" I said, looking up at him in response.

"Is everything okay?" John said, concerned.

"Yes," I said. "There is a lot of work with exams coming up."

"I understand," John said with his eyes lowered.

I wondered if Ibrahim had said something to him. I wondered if my best friend had already lost her stated resolve to retain my personal information as my confidante. I wondered if John thought less of me. For some reason, I cared about what John thought. He was a decent human being, and I wanted decent human beings to have a good opinion of me.

"We never have time to talk," I said to break the ice.

"Well, I am sure that Ibrahim is more interesting than me," John said and gave me a friendly wink and a smile.

"Seriously, we should talk more often," I said, quite at a loss as what to say.

"I have to confess that what times we had the pleasure of sharing conversation, I enjoyed very much."

"Me, too," I added. "One question has been bugging me for awhile. Can I ask you?"

"Shoot!" he said in a light-hearted way.

"Why did you come to Israel? There are so many nice places in the world."

John looked at me seriously for awhile. I felt that he was analyzing me to see if he could trust me or not.

"Okay, I will tell you," John said at last. "Like yourself, I am a Christian," John continued. "I am a Baptist and proud to be."

"What is a Baptist?" I asked. "Is that like being a Catholic?"

"Baptists believe that you must believe that Jesus is God and be born again in the Spirit to have eternal life."

"That's what we Catholics believe, too," I replied.

"Yes, I know," John said. "There are ignorant people out there who try to put a wedge between Baptists and Catholics, but Jesus said that Kingdom divided against itself cannot stand. Those who believe Jesus as God must stand together."

I remained silent because he sounded serious, and the fiery tone frankly frightened me.

"I guess, what I am trying to say," John said in a lowered, calmer voice, "is that I agree with the decision of the Southern Baptist Convention that we need to show love towards the Jews by converting them to Christianity, so that they will not go to eternal Hell-fire."

"You mean, you came all the way to Israel to convert Jews?" I said in surprise.

"Well, I figured that it'll take time," John said. "If the Baptists are to convert all the Jews to Christianity, then we'll have to know about them, first."

"You are being serious!" I said, quite shocked. Catholics were not into converting Jews, and I felt good about that because I knew that they would get what they deserved for oppressing Arabs – eternal damnation in Hell. I was a bit disappointed that John liked the Jews so much.

"That's why I started the Christian Union, here," John said. "But I'm afraid we only have Gentiles from America now. It doesn't seem like that will change any time soon, unfortunately."

"Well, good luck," I said because I felt that it was the right thing to say.

I was beginning to feel uncomfortable with all the holy talk. It seemed to distance him from me. I wanted John to be my friend, so I changed the subject.

"So, do you have a girlfriend back home?" I asked.

"Yes," John said abruptly. After a second's pause he continued, "Actually, no."

"What do you mean?"

"She broke up with me," John said.

"What happened?" I asked, curious.

"A friend of mine at church and she developed a bond," John replied with emptiness in his voice.

"In your absence?" I blurted out.

"She's no Penelope," John said, sarcastically. Then, quickly, he added, "He is a good guy at least."

"I'm sorry to hear that," I said.

"That's okay," John said. "Listen, I'm sorry, but I better get back to work."

"Okay," I said, feeling bad for him. "But if you ever need to talk, please feel free to call me anytime."

"Thanks," John said and left.

I sat there feeling sad. John was such a good guy, and he lost his girlfriend because they were apart. I wondered what created the distance between John and his girlfriend. How did she ever manage to make the emotional break from someone she loved? It did not seem right that John was hurting. He did not deserve to hurt.

For the next few days, I thought about John and his pain. I worked hard, especially because Ibrahim was no longer in the city. Ibrahim's mom became sick, and he left in a hurry. I tried to comfort him over the phone, but I felt terrible that I could not comfort him in person. I felt bad and guilty for staying away from him. I felt that I was unfair to him and resolved to tell him when he returned from his home.

To atone for my guilt, I resolved to go to his room and clean up his room. I did not know what else to do, and I felt that that would ease my conscience.

When I knocked on the door, John answered. It looked like he's been crying. I quickly looked away and created an awkward moment unintentionally.

"Welcome in," John said sheepishly like one who had been caught stealing a cookie out of granny's cookie jar.

"Thanks," I said.

I looked at him and realized that I could not just abruptly say goodbye and go into Ibrahim's room. I threw out my original plan to clean Ibrahim's room and surprise him. Instead, I decided to be a good friend to John in his time of need.

"It's good to see you," I said.

"Yes, it is," John responded, while trying to capture his composure.

"Ibrahim keeps some good tea from Saudi Arabia," I said. "Would you like to share it with me?"

"Thanks," John said, seemingly comforted. "That would be great."

John and I talked over tea. We talked and talked. I was surprised to discover how deep he was as a person. I had thought that he was nice, but a bit superficial. But this time talking showed me how wrong I had been. It felt like discovering an apple tree in Ashkelon.

Minutes turned into hours, and I knew that it was getting really late. As much as I hated to, I knew that it would be proper to say goodbye.

"Wow, time flies when you are having fun," I said.

"I can't believe how late it is," John replied.

"I better go back home," I said.

"Please, allow me to accompany you," John said, looking worried. It was late.

"No, that's okay," I said. "I can handle myself."

I was a bit worried though, and I was sure that it showed through.

"Ibrahim is not here, but I know that he'll trust you with his room," John said, looking more worried. "Why don't you stay in his room, if you won't let me accompany you back home. It is very late."

"I guess, you are right," I said.

John bid me goodnight and went to his room and left the whole palace to me. I appreciated his consideration, and felt comfortable staying in Ibrahim's room. I realized how tired and restless I had been. In a few minutes I was sound asleep in the security of Ibrahim's room.

When I woke the next morning, it was quite late. I walked outside the room and found a note from John. It read: "Good morning! Help yourself to anything and everything in the fridge."

It was so casual, so familiar, that I felt like I had known John my whole life. I obeyed the order and helped myself to the best breakfast I had in a long time. I had missed morning classes but felt refreshed for afternoon ones. The day turned out to be without a blemish.

I didn't know what was keeping Ibrahim. He did not return for a couple of weeks. He did not like the phone, so he did not call often. Few times he called, I was at the university, so I missed the calls. I did not dare call him back because his parents did not know about me.

I continued to visit Ibrahim's room and shared conversations with John. I expressed my concerns and worries about Ibrahim and his mother. John offered words of Jesus as comfort. At first, I felt quite weird about it, but John's friendly demeanor made it more and more natural.

I appreciated John for his dedication to his faith. I wish I had that. I found that he and my mother were quite alike in their Christian faith and outlook, and this endeared him to me more. John was never judgmental, but he was always engaged and offered the Christian perspective. Having grown up in a Christian home, this was strangely comforting.

In two week's time, word came back from Ibrahim. It was bad news. His mom had passed away. Ibrahim was completely devastated as he treasured her above all else.

When Ibrahim returned, he seemed distant and lost. No words of comfort seemed to encourage him. I felt that it was a natural reaction and with time he would recover. I hoped that his old self would return and that he would be the same old strong Ibrahim that I had fallen in love with.

Weeks passed and passed, but there was no recovery. I felt totally helpless. To make matters worse, I found out that he was experimenting with drugs. Ibrahim never ever touched a cigarette in his life before, and now he was puffing away at mind-blowing agents.

Then, one day, Ibrahim said to me, "You know I love you, right?"

"Yes, of course," I said.

"But I have to find myself," Ibrahim said.

"Find yourself?" I asked, surprised.

"Jenny. I have decided to go to Tibet for one year and embark on a spiritual journey."

"Are you serious?" I exclaimed. I was disturbed by his rashness.

"Jenny, I am sorry, but this is not up for discussion," Ibrahim said.

I was shocked. I wanted to shake him and tell him to be the strong Arab male that was needed in Israel. I wanted to slap him around and command him to wake up from his self-pity. I wanted to tell him straight to his face to be a man. But I faltered. I knew instinctively that I had to let him go.

Trying to suppress tears welling up in my eyes, I said, "I don't want you to go, and if you go, I can't wait for you."

I was secretly hoping that this would change his mind. After all, he loved me, didn't he?

"Jenny, I am sorry," Ibrahim said. "But I can't stay. I am sorry."

Ibrahim left and that was the last that I saw of him. John told me that he left the next day for Tibet. Apparently, he had already purchased the plane ticket before coming to talk to me. I felt betrayed, although I knew that he was not my possession. I thought we were in a relationship and he owed me a little more than what he gave me at the end.

John was a good friend and comforted me without explicitly talking about what happened. I enjoyed tea times with John and began to attend the Christian Union meetings that he had started.

By the time that the end of his one year came around the Christian Union grew to 30 people. John located some more "lost souls" among American students. I brought some Arab Christian friends. And two Messianic Jews, who believed in the deity of Jesus but refused to call themselves Christians, came. John was disappointed that no Jew was converted to Christianity, but he said that he was sure that the ground work was laid and that the harvest will be gathered in the future.

Now, you may be wondering what happened between John and me. Did we stay friends? Did anything romantic develop? The conclusion to John's one-year stay in Israel provided the strangest ending.

A week before he was due to depart for the USA, John asked me out to dinner. He was his friendly self and made the dinner seem like a nice goodbye dinner. Without hesitation, I accepted the invitation.

Half-way into the dinner, John got down on his knees and asked me to marry him! It was so sudden and out of the blue. It was a complete shock.

John said that he loved me the first time he saw me and that he knew that it was God's will that we marry and devote ourselves to missions to the Jews. He seemed so convinced of our future together that it was hard for me to say, "No."

But, as wonderful as John was and as much as I liked him, I did not know if I could marry him. I did not know if I loved him.

But more important than that, I did not like John's plan for our lives. He wanted to convert Jews to Christianity. Perhaps, John could find it in his heart to love Jews enough to give them the opportunity to belong to the family of Christ. I wasn't.

Jews have tortured Arabic people in Israel. I personally know many people who suffered at the hands of Jews, and I even know some who died at their hands unjustly, albeit legally under the unfair Israeli law. I wanted all Jews to go to Hell. I did not want to have to face a day when Jews were to go and spend eternity in heaven with me. Two messianic Jews, who apparently looked down on Gentiles enough to refuse the title "Christian", were enough Jews going to heaven that I needed to know. I knew that having to share the Gospel with Jews would be a Hell on earth for me, so I rejected John's proposal.

Now, I am in Israel working with the Palestinian Authority to lobby against unjust laws of the State of Israel. There is talk that I will be selected to represent Palestine in the United Nations.

The last time I heard, John was ordained in a Southern Baptist church after finishing his seminary studies at Dallas Theological Seminary. At the Seminary, John met a Messianic Jew, who wants all Jews converted to Christianity, fell in love, and married her.

I don't know if she uses the title "Christian" for herself or not, but John writes that he is very happy and sent a wedding photo. His wife, Shoshanna, looks beautiful. And I have a feeling that she is the right person for him.

What happened to Ibrahim? Ibrahim spent two years in Tibet and became a Buddhist monk. He is one of the very few Arabic Buddhist monks running around in the world, I would imagine. Interestingly enough, his closest friend is an American orthodox Jew who became a Buddhist monk. They met the first day of Ibrahim's arrival in Tibet and have been best of friends since. Both Ibrahim's and David's families have declared their son "dead."

Ibrahim writes that he has never been more alive in his life and vows to bring the good news of Buddhism to Israel in the future with his friend David.

Jewish and Indian

My name is Hadas Ashkenazi, and I am an Indian Jew. My family lives in the Negev in a community of Indian Jews. We as a community produce and sell flowers all over Israel, and recently we have started expanding our business to sell flowers abroad.

My family, like other Indian families in the community, immigrated to Israel several decades ago. The State of Israel was allowing immigration under the Law of Return, and my family took the opportunity to leave Kochin and India behind. Now, there are hardly any Indian Jews over there. All have left, many ending up in Israel. The synagogue still stands there, but it's now empty, from what I hear.

I was born in Israel, so I could be called a Sabra. But I have to confess that I feel different. Sometimes, I feel the loneliness of not belonging. It seems that I am different from Sabras and the way they live.

I do have to confess that I was embarrassed to bring my friends over. We Indians in Israel eat different food. We eat Indian food. Since most Indian Jews are from Kochin, we consume Indian food from that area in India. India is a big country from what I hear, and my mom tells me that it is beautiful. There are many different regional traditions and cuisines, but Indians feel united in a way. I have to confess that I can only imagine what she means because I have never had the opportunity to visit India. I have only lived in Israel, and hold what is here as my standard and guide.

I don't know what is in India and that may be the reason why it is difficult for me to take pride in India or my Indian heritage. My parents' fond reminiscences of India do not make sense to me. As I look at the glow in their eyes, I wish I could feel what they feel. I wish I had a sense of belonging that they seem to have.

I live in Israel with my fellow Jews. In school, they always emphasize that we are one people. All Jews are one. But I don't feel that I am the same. I eat different food every day. I eat Indian food, and I like it.

My parents are not like the parents of my Israeli friends. They talk differently and have different gestures. They shake their heads side ways often, and none of the Israeli people whom I know do that. Whenever we are in public, I am really self-conscious that they will do these Indian expressions. I am afraid that Israelis will burst out with laughter.

My parents could hardly speak Hebrew before coming to Israel. After immigration, they took the mandatory modern Hebrew classes because the prevalent idea in Israel is that Jews are one and Hebrew is the language of the Jews. All immigrants are mandated to learn Hebrew and speak Hebrew. Speaking in other languages is actively discouraged. It may be because the framers of modern Hebrew in the State of Israel were French that such aggressive push for assimilation exists here. From what I understand, France holds French culture as the single standard for France and expects anyone holding French citizenship to assimilate into French ways.

It is ironic that the State of Israel has adopted such an aggressive assimilationist policy that some Jews in Europe fought against. Some of the books I read in school make French people out to be anti-semitic because they expected Jews in France to adopt French ways and be one of them.

Now, we are here in Israel as immigrants, and we are expected to conform in the same way. I see a double standard and sometimes complain to my parents. But although they do not speak Hebrew very well or understand Israeli ways fully, they are nationalists and Zionists. They tell me that it should be that way. They tell me that they want me to be no different from other Israelis.

They tell me that they did not teach me to write any Indian languages because they want me to be one of them, the Israelis. But I see a contradiction. My parents still speak to me in their Indian language. I guess it's comfortable for them. I can clearly see that they value their Indian heritage. So, I have questions. Why don't they want me to share that part of their experience? I know they love me, but sometimes I wonder about how much. I feel left out when mom and dad talk because I don't understand the inside jokes.

I know that I feel different here in Israel, and I am sure that my parents feel different, too. They are not particularly religious, and that is okay since many of my Israeli friends are secular and don't care about religion. But I see myself and my family as different from most Israelis. And I have to raise the question of why my parents immigrated to Israel. Obviously, they speak with fondness about India. And they hardly have non-Indian friends.

The more I think about it, I feel that they immigrated for economic reasons. India, from the pictures I have seen in my school textbooks, seems like a poor country. Israel is a wealthy country by comparison.

And I am becoming more and more convinced that Zionist loyalty that they exhibit is just an act. They don't believe it, but they act Zionist because they are now in Israel. It is expected of them. Since as immigrants from India they are different from other Israelis, they must have suffered racism from Israelis for being different. And they must have been expected to show their loyalty to the State of Israel. They know that I have to be a loyal Zionist to get ahead in

Israel, so they are going out of their way to educate me as a Zionist so that no one will question my loyalty to Israel. I can be accepted in Israel this way.

But I am different just like they are different. Even if I speak without an Indian accent, I know that Israelis see me differently. How many Asians are there in Israel? Less than .0001 per cent. Who has Indian food at home regularly, except for the few Indian Jews in our community and in other small communities?

I guess that I can't blame my parents for moving here. I am sure that I would not have had the opportunities that I have here if we had not moved here. Probably not. I should be grateful to my parents. After all, my struggles probably do not compare to the sacrifices that they have made, especially seeing that they clearly miss India.

And in most cases, I don't think that the Israelis are intentionally being cruel to me because I am Indian. There's probably one or two who may be intentionally unkind to me, but that's just human nature. It's probably their ignorance about my culture and my experience of growing up in an Indian home that confuses them. The food we eat is not Jewish or Israeli, in the sense popularly understood. And most Israelis will live a life-time without meeting one Indian Jew, since there are only few of us. So, their awkwardness when faced with an Indian Jew is understandable.

The problem for me is that this knowledge is not comforting. Although I can understand why they might behave in an unkind way, it doesn't make me feel any better. It does not help in my effort to understand myself and my identity as an Indian and a Jew.

Certainly, the State of Israel's discouraging exploration of such an identity does not help matters. You are an Israeli, and you must be happy and satisfied with that identity. But I am not. The older I become, I feel that my Indian identity becomes more and more important. Perhaps, it's a kind of self-realization. Maybe I am made to think more about it as other Israelis make me feel different, whether consciously or unconsciously.

But I feel that I am caught between a rock and a hard place. My parents made a decisive break with India. What their reasons truly were, I don't honestly know. But they have made no concerted effort to visit the country. We have not had any visitors from India, either. I don't know any of my relatives in India. I don't know where I can start to explore my Indian identity.

There are hardly any Indians here in Israel, and there are not resources to explore Indian culture. You can hardly find Indian restaurants. There just isn't the interest in India.

So, how can I understand myself and who I am? Should I resign myself to an Israeli identity cast upon me by my surrounding, education, friends at school, and even my parents? It should be the easiest thing to do. I can forget my Indian culture and heritage. I could just blend in.

But I know that I can't go through with it. I can't because I am unable to stop eating Indian food. I can't stop appreciating little things that are distinctively Indian in culture which I picked up from my parents. Short anecdotes about India that I hear from my parents have become a part of my identity, and I cannot deny their place in my self-perception and identity.

What am I to do in my state of isolation? I am an Indian and a Jew. I am alone in this country with people who cannot begin to understand what that means.

To be honest, I don't feel a particular affinity to Israeli culture and its values. First of all, since I am not religious, I do not feel a belonging to the religious population in Israel. Perhaps, if I were religious, I would find greater association and identity within the Israeli context. But I am not religious. I do not believe that Moses passed down the Oral Law that has been preserved for thousands of years. It sounds ridiculous to me. If that were true, then there would be Jews who could recite the Oral Law by heart without the text in front of them. But I have heard of no religious Jew who could do this. If religious Jews of today can't preserve the Oral Law from mouth to mouth without writing it down, then obviously religious Jews of the past couldn't do it either. Religious Judaism seems dishonest and that hinders my considering being orthodox. And I will not become a religious Jew just to find social acceptance. I cannot lie to myself and be happy.

So, I am left with exploring a secular identity. As much as secular Jews want to claim that they are inclusive and tolerant, they are not. Look at the way secular Jews hate religious Jews.

Some secular Jews hate religious Jews more than they hate Syrians. And Israel and Syria are in a state of impending war.

If these secular Jews are intolerant of religious Jews and reject them and their rights to be religious, why should I find acceptance among these secular Jews? Although I am not religious, I am different from them. I eat different food, my parents act strangely by social conventions of Israeli culture, and I have darker skin than most Israelis, just to cite a few factors. I could try to ingratiate myself in the secular Israeli camp, but that would mean I have to turn my back on my past. I am not willing to turn my back on my Indian identity and experiences treasured by my parents.

As much as my parents encourage me to abandon myself to the larger Israeli culture, they don't really understand what they are asking for. My abandoning Indian culture will necessitate my rejection of them! If I turn my back on India, I turn my back on my parents. Don't they realize that they are Indians? They don't go to a synagogue. They don't even fast on Yom Kippur. There is nothing about them that makes them Jews, really. They were born into religious Jewish families. My dad had a Bar Mitzvah. They were married in a synagogue. But neither of them believe in Judaism, now. They don't practice any of the Mitzvoth. They are not Kosher. They drive on the Sabbath. And I have seem them eat pork in Eilat. They are not Jews in the religious sense. And they are not Israelis in the cultural sense. They are Indians. I don't know how they could continue living a lie and pretending that they are Jews. They have an Israeli citizenship, but they are Indians.

If I reject my Indian heritage, how can I get myself to respect my parents and look at them in the face. A large part of why I respect them and love them is because I know them and their values. Their values are Indian. Their memories are transcribed through the eyes of Indians. How could they not understand that the reason why my Israeli friends giggle at them is because their mannerisms are distinctively Indian?

I refuse to turn my back on India and thereby turn my back on my parents. I know I am not a part of Judaism. I don't even feel like I am Israeli. If I abandoned one thing that gives me a semblance of identity, I will be a person without an identity.

It's all nice and well for an Ashkenazi Jew abandoning his French heritage. There are so many French Jews in Israel. Food that they eat in Israel will have a lot of similarities with what they ate in France.

But an Indian Jew? We are different. We do different things. We eat different things. We have a different culture.

Anyone who says that there is a homogeneous Jewish culture is a liar. If that were the case, then a Jew from England should feel completely at home in an Indian Jew's home. They won't. English Jews and Indian Jews are fundamentally different culturally.

An English Jew will feel more comfortable with an English Gentile than with an Indian Jew because English Jews share English culture with English Gentiles. There is no such thing as a Jewish culture, particularly if you are secular.

I know for fact that I would feel more comfortable with an Indian Gentile who has mannerisms like my parents and eat the same kind of food that I do. I wouldn't have to feel embarrassed when my parents wave their head side to side. I wouldn't have to feel apologetic about Indian food and its exotic spices. Since I have no loyalty to Judaism, there is no religious barrier. Any way, I understand that Hindus are tolerant. They will accept me as I am, while religious Jews will not.

I will hold fast to my Indian culture and explore my Indian identity. I will read more about India and will try to find opportunities to meet more Indians.

Most importantly, I have to leave Israel. Israel is not a place for an Indian and a Jew like me. I am rejected because I am an Indian. And I am rejected because I am not really religiously Jewish.

I cannot feel anything when talks of anti-semitism abound. Jews lived a happy life in India. Indian Jews never felt a need to found a Jewish state. The idea of a Jewish nation as something important makes no sense to me. I consider myself as a secular citizen of the world. I belong to the world community. I am not confined and do not want to be imprisoned in a singular identity imposed on me.

I have to leave Israel because I am really not Jewish and do not feel comfortable with Israelis who don't understand India. And I don't want to limit myself to this small Indian community in the Negev. I want to be free to go wherever and work and live. I want to be in a place where I can find Indians in large numbers and have access to Indian food. I can chuck away my Jewish identity since I am not religious. I cannot identify myself with secular Zionism of Theodore Herzl. I cannot understand all the hatred that Ashkenazi Jews have toward Gentiles. It is not a part of my history and experience. Having lived all my life in Israel as an Indian, I resent hostility I have experienced from Ashkenazi Jews who don't understand Indian culture. Any racism or discrimination I have experienced in my life came from Jews and not from Gentiles. I don't even know that many Gentiles. Those Gentiles that I do know have been kind and friendly. All this talk of anti-semitism does not make sense to me. It's not a part of my experience.

I will go to England. That is what I will do because England has a large Indian community, which will accept me. I look like them. I eat their food. I share their history going back thousands of years. Indians in England will not judge me for my Indian ways and make me feel like an outsider.

And since my English is fluent, I would be able to communicate with them and share common culture with them. I would be able to explore my Indian identity without feeling like I am committing a crime.

I am not a Jew. I don't believe. I don't practice. For me, being Israeli is just a citizenship. I will have no problem changing my citizenship to an English one. I am me, Hadas Ashkenazi. I want to be loved for being me. I want to be loved as Hadas and not as something that Israelis want me to be. I want to be free. I want to be free as Hadas. I want to be Hadas, who is happy and free. I want to be Hadas, who is free to explore my identity as an Indian. I want to be me.

Neutralize

"We have to figure out a way to neutralize him," Saul said.

"Mr. Steinberg, how do you propose we do that?" Adam retorted.

"My dear Mr. Wolfberg, it's quite simple, really." Saul smiled and said, "You see, you have to apply the principle of divide and conquer."

"And how do you suppose we do that?" Adam asked, curious.

Saul continued, "You see, we infiltrate his social environment."

"Social environment?"

"Yes, his social association, such as the nice little Christian Union he goes to. After all, he's a Christian as well."

A sinister smile came over Adam's face.

Saul became excited, "First, you put one of our own in the Christian Union. Or maybe more than one. You can send someone who seems interested in the Christian faith. It will all be pretend, of course, but these naïve Christians who don't know the evils of the world won't know that."

"I see, a wolf in a sheep's clothing," Adam said excitedly.

"Precisely, my dear Mr. Wolfberg," Saul said, self-satisfied. "Christians will bend over backwards and forwards to help this convert, and he, or she, will win their hearts and souls."

"Over from Christ," Adam interjected.

"Without their knowing, of course," Saul smiled. "The Christian Union is so desperate for members as it shrinks in size that they will fall into our hands blindly," Saul explained. "The Jew pretending to be a Christian convert can go to every Christian Union meeting so he, or she, can convince Christians that his, or her, conversion is genuine. After all, Christians judge by appearances. Don't you know the saying by Christians? 'You shall know them by their fruit.' What we'll do is show the fruit. Attending Christian services and behaving like a goody-goody should not be hard."

Adam added, "And we can pay our little spy. It'll be like the Jewish scholarship fund to infiltrate the Christian camp."

"Yes, to protect Jewish interests," Saul agreed. "And they are naïve. Christians have proven time after time how gullible they are. We'll pick a Jew with a non-Jewish name, perhaps with a Gentile father and a Jewish mother. In most cases, these Jews become more loyal to Judaism because the Gentile-marrying Jewish mother will try to compensate for her guilt by imbuing her children with overzealousness for Jewish things."

Adam said approvingly. "Yes, intermarriage works for us in these cases. We know how dominant Jewish women are. A WASP or Catholic husband cannot influence his children over a Jewess."

Saul replied, "Yes, I agree. Our women are something, although I have to confess that I prefer Gentile women myself because Jewish women are too dominant."

Adam criticized, "The Schiksa factor. Your mother would not approve."

Saul waved off Adam's comments. "What does my preference for Gentile women matter? I will just force them to convert to Judaism before marriage."

Adam corrected, "Persuade, please."

Saul said, "I know you don't like Jewish men dating Gentile women. You have been brainwashed by the intermarriage-as-genocide theory. Think of it this way. If you convert a Gentile, you would actually go the other way."

Adam said, "I don't like it."

Saul replied, "I know you are a purist. But let's keep to the issue at hand."

Adam protested, "You digressed."

Saul responded, "You are right. You are right."

Adam relented, "Okay."

Saul stated, "Yes, the security of the Jewish people is at stake and that's what's really important."

Adam added, "And not to mention the security of the Jewish State of Israel."

Saul replied, "Isn't that one and the same thing?"

Adam chided, "Oh, you Schiksa-loving secular Zionist! You will be the death of us all."

Saul said, "Can we stick to the subject?"

Adam said, "Okay, you are right."

Saul continued, "So, we'll infiltrate the debilitated Christian Union. If we can pay a smart first-year student to be a model convert, then by the third year, he'll be leading Bible study groups of the Christian Union."

Adam expressed his doubt, "Christians can't be that stupid."

Saul nodded, "Believe me. Christians are that stupid. It may be because these naïve Christians grew up in Christian homes away from the world, but they don't know how the world operates. Trust me."

Adam replied gleefully, "It'll be like our own Judas Iscariot."

Saul said pensively, "That's something else we can consider."

"What?"

Saul answered, "Judas was bought. We can buy someone in the Christian Union."

Adam questioned, "Buy?"

Saul answered, "As a matter of speaking. You know how the KGB bought CIA agents."

Adam responded, "I see. Like we get a nice Jewish girl to influence a Christian guy."

Saul explained, "He won't need to know that she's Jewish. But the main thrust of the idea is there."

Adam chimed in, "Most of these Christian guys are virgins and they won't know what hit them. Once they taste the forbidden fruit, they will not be able to control themselves. They will sell out Christ quicker than you can say, 'Christian.'"

Saul commented, "I see that you are getting into the spirit of things."

Adam replied, "You are an evil master-mind. Glad you are on the Jewish side and not on Christians'."

Saul stated authoritatively, "Christians have a bunch of naïve people who don't know the world or the ways of the world. But you know as well as I that this is not true for Jews. We have anti-semitism all around us, so we don't trust anybody. It makes us wiser in the ways of the world. And we can use it to our advantage."

Adam replied, "The Christian Union won't know what hit them."

Saul said, "Before you know it, we'll have naïve Christians fighting our battles for us."

Adam said, "Self-destruction. I like that."

Saul commented, "But let's focus on the primary mission."

Adam responded, "Yes. Neutralization."

Saul explained, "If we can neutralize him then nothing else will matter."

Adam said, "You mean all those Christians don't matter?"

Saul said, "They are all ignorant. They don't know like he knows. If we can neutralize him, then they will continue in their ignorance. We can continue to do our thing, and we'll be secure."

"But, if he gains forum, then we are fucked."

"Yes," Saul concurred. "So, it's our primary objective to neutralize him."

Adam said, "So, we'll send in a paid convert, and we'll try to infiltrate the Christian Union with KGB-like tactics."

Saul interrupted, "That's not all. First of all, we'll do that not only for the Christian Union but for the Baptist church that he attends."

Adam said, "And you are saying that Christians will not be able to detect what we are doing?"

Saul said, "How are a bunch of people who don't know the world going to find out? They don't understand us Jews, our hopes and fears. Besides, they will eventually become so dependent on our people, for instance, for running their programs and events, that they will trust our people over true Christians."

Adam replied, "It must have been easy to get Jesus Christ killed. Is naiveté the characteristic of Christians?"

Saul said, "They say love, but I would say naiveté. If love were so important, then we would not be able to segregate a true Christian from his camp. But you see, Christians are naïve and self-righteous. They judge based on one's actions. That's their Achilles' heel – their emphasis on the appearance. We'll just fabricate actions and attendance at Christian events for our people, and we'll have them."

Adam smiled and said, "It sounds so easy."

Saul confirmed, "Trust me. It is. I have done years of research into this subject. I could probably win a prize if I published my findings, but I know it would give away the secret. I want to help our Jewish community, so I won't."

Adam said, "You are a true Jewish nationalist."

Saul said, "We Jews have to stick together. If we don't , evil will befall us."

Adam commented, "It's great that Christians won't stick together. Their being idiots helps the Jewish cause."

Saul said, "So, we'll neutralize Peter."

Adam replied, "That fucking Palestinian bastard!"

Saul exhorted, "Don't get emotional. We'll use his Christian brothers and sisters to kill him – so to speak. And remember that he is a person of color."

Adam nodded, "I see."

Saul continued, "You know how white Christians prefer Jews who are white rather than blacks or Hispanic Christians? White Christians don't respect Christians of color as they do other whites, even if we are Jews. So, we'll use that weakness to our advantage."

Adam exclaimed, "Brilliant! Using the sinful nature of white Christians to kill off a Christian of color."

"Divide and conquer," Saul confirmed.

"And Jesus himself said that a kingdom divided against itself cannot stand," Adam said.

"That's what I like about you. You know your enemy," Saul complimented.

"You know how many Jews are teaching the New Testament in Ivy League universities? Do you think that they are loyal to Christians or to Jews?"

"To Jews, of course," Saul said emphatically.

"We have Jews teaching the New Testament to Christians in universities. You see how naïve Christians are for allowing us to do this. Do you think that Jews, if we had power, would allow Christians to teach Judaism?"

"Certainly, not," Saul answered the rhetorical question.

"Brandeis hiring a devout Catholic to teach Judaism. That would mean the end of the world," Adam said.

Saul replied, "We Jews are not that stupid. We know the world. We know all Gentiles are anti-semitic."

Adam replied, "We must remember that."

Saul said, "Yes, we will not forget. We will remember."

"We must not forget that we must destroy him and his kind," Adam said.

"Yes, we must remember," Saul affirmed.

Adam said, "He knows too much and his people respect him."

Saul said, "That is why he is dangerous. And that is why our plan is important. It'll work and it'll destroy him and his kind. It's either them or us."

Adam repeated, "Them or us."

"Let's hash out the details later," Saul suggested.

"Okay, that sounds good," Adam agreed. "I need to go, too."

Saul waived goodbye and said, "See you later."

Saul and Adam left their little corner, smiling.

A few minutes later Peter entered the same cafeteria. He was talking to a friend from the university.

Peter said, "Yeah, I really enjoyed studying at Haifa University."

David replied, "Really? What did you like about it?"

Peter commented, "I liked the fact that the professors seemed understanding of my ideas."

David asked inquisitively, "What idea is that?"

Peter answered, "I believe that the Palestinian state is feasible and good for both Palestinians and Jews."

David replied, "Isn't that what everyone in the world thinks?"

Peter replied, "You mean the positions of the United Nations and the USA? Yes, that's their official position. But I think most people don't think about it seriously. Certainly, people in Israel don't agree with that position, particularly under the current Prime Minister."

David said, "But you are saying that you found professors who agreed with your position?"

"Yes, I did," Peter replied. "They were more open-minded. And I think they are being smart. There is no way that there is going to be peace in the Middle East unless there is a peaceful co-existence through the founding of the Palestinian state."

David commented, "It sounds like you are serious about this."

Peter said, "I believe that Palestinian people should not lie down and let Israel trample upon us. Or carry out assassinations of our leaders when we are in the middle of an UN-supported peace process. But I do want peace between our peoples. Since Jews stole our land away from us less than 100 years ago, I don't think I am asking too much when I say we should share land. In fact, I think I am being generous."

David replied, "If it means peace in the Middle East, I am all for it. Peace in the Middle East will mean security for Americans."

Survival

"Is it really important that Jews survive as Jews or Jews survive as individuals?"

"What kind of question is that?"

"Well, you know how some Jewish leaders are saying that Jews need to survive as Jews and that Jewish people have a common identity and destiny?"

"Yeah."

"But consider this, if Jews completely reject their Jewish identity, religious or otherwise, and completely assimilate into the larger context to the extent that even their children almost do not know that they are Jews, what's wrong with that?"

"But Jewish identity is important!"

"Why is Jewish identity so important? Isn't survival more important? If emphasizing Jewishness actually brings danger to Jewish individuals, then isn't Jewishness the problem?"

"No, anti-semitism is!"

"But it takes two to tango. If Jews did not emphasize that they are Jewish, why would they experience anti-semitism? Anti-semitism exists because Jews continuously impose ourselves on the larger context. Anti-semitism is a natural reaction to imposition."

"Now, you are speaking like an anti-semite."

"Your throwing that title around is not constructive at all to the discussion. Will the term stop violence? It will probably unite the Other against us. Does the term help us to solve problems? No. It's not a constructive term but rather a destructive term."

"What do you propose?"

"I would propose that Jews focus on being a part of the humanity. Jews should not portray ourselves as misanthropes by working hard to set ourselves apart from the rest of humanity. Creating division is an action that will encourage reaction. In Hegelian terms, emphasizing Jewishness and the need for Jewish identity is the thesis and there will be an opposite reaction in the extreme. The end result is synthesis."

"So you are saying that anti-semitism is the synthesis?"

"No. Emphasizing Jewishness is the thesis. The anti-semitic response is the antithesis. Synthesis is something like the pogroms or the holocaust."

"That sounds irrational. You are saying, encouraging Jewishness actually invites violence against Jews."

"Yes. It is only natural. When people are living in a community and a few keep segregating themselves apart from the commonality of the larger community, they invite resentment and even violence."

"Let me understand you correctly. You are saying that if Jews did not emphasize Jewishness, then Jews can escape violence."

"Precisely. You can't be a target if you don't have a delineable, identifiable group. A group can only be targeted if a group exists."

"So you are saying pogroms in Russia happened because Jews emphasized Jewishness?"

"Yes. If Russia's Jews assimilated then they would not have brought attention on themselves."

"So you are also saying that the holocaust happened because Jews emphasized Jewishness?"

"Yes, most certainly. Isn't it too much of a coincidence that the greatest violence against Jews happened when greatest Jewish nationalism manifested itself in Europe?"

"What? That's ridiculous!"

"Why is it ridiculous? The Zionists are to be blamed for the holocaust. If German Jews were allowed to assimilate and thrive without Zionist discourse imposing itself on the non-Jewish world, Jews would not have been targeted."

"But haven't you heard of the 'failure of assimilation'?"

"What failure? The one caused by ethnocentric Zionists?"

"How about the Dreyfus Affair? Isn't it a good example of how an assimilated Jew can be persecuted just because he is Jewish?"

"No. I think the Dreyfus Affair is blown way out of proportion by the Zionists. Also, it is an isolated case. Maybe the fact that the Zionists made a big deal about it and started accusing the French of anti-semitism actually caused an expected response."

"You are blaming Jews for anti-semitism?"

"Hey, you sound like I am a traitor to my people. I am trying to offer a constructive discourse for Jewish survival. There is a reason why Jews keep getting killed, kicked out, or attacked in different countries with different languages and cultures. It's about time that Jews don't take the easy road out and blame everything on anti-semitism. It's not a constructive solution for future Jewish survival."

"So, what do you propose?"

"I say, we must go against the creation of the thesis that invites or even propels the response of the antithesis."

"You are saying we must not emphasize Jewishness."

"Precisely. We must go back to the assimilationist model that was making progress until a bunch of disillusioned, backward Eastern European Jews invaded Western Europe with their Zionist ideas."

"That's a bit harsh!"

"It's true. Assimilating Western Europeans were enjoying unprecedented power and acceptance in Europe and Eastern European Jews who had problems in their backyard brought their problems to our backyard. And 6 million Jews were killed because a few disenchanted Eastern European Jews went on a rampage of discontent and imposed Jewishness on the Gentile world. What do you expect? If you introduce a thesis, you will get an antithesis, resulting in a synthesis."

"It's not fair. Jews are innocent."

"We are not talking about innocence or guilt. We are talking about survival. Is it more important to impose the Jewish right on the Gentile world even if it means pogroms? For myself, I rather have Jewish survival."

"But it is by morally stating that we are right and that anti-semitism is wrong that Jews will survive."

"My friend, you have been living in an academic bubble too long. Do you think that an average person in the street cares about these moral issues as we call them? You separate Jews from the larger group, we Jews become targets. That's what Eastern European Zionists did to us."

"Should you not be blaming the anti-semites rather than fellow Jews who have good intentions?"

"What do good intentions mean if my children are killed in a pogrom? I can't control Gentiles, but I figure that I have a better chance of influencing the Jewish community as a member of the in-group."

"No Jew will listen to you."

"Yeah, that's the Jewish tragedy. That's why Jews keep getting killed at the height of their prosperity. Alexandria. Spain. Russia. Germany. Need I say more?"

"You are now making it sound like you are not even Jewish!"

"Let me be honest with you. I am not religiously Jewish. I'm secular. I don't observe any of the Jewish customs. Why should I die because some disgruntled Zionists want to make an imposition on the larger Gentile world? I think it's important that I live as a human being. It's not important to me that I live as a Jew."

"So, you are a self-hating Jew!"

"Sticks and stones, my friend. Sticks and stones."

"You are going to turn your back on your people."

"What are you talking about? I am an English citizen who lived most of his life in America. I could consider myself English, and possibly American. English people are my people. Let me ask you. What makes you particularly Jewish?"

"I fast on Yom Kippur."

"So, you consider yourself religiously Jewish?"

"Well, no. I actually feel like I am culturally Jewish."

"What the hell does that mean? Culturally Jewish? What does that mean?"

"Well, I see myself as being a part of Jewish culture."

"See, you can't even explain yourself. You do everything that Gentiles do. Maybe you fast on Yom Kippur, have a watered down Seder, give presents in Hanukah. That's not enough to say you are culturally Jewish. You have been brainwashed by the Zionists."

"I don't think you are right."

"Okay. Let me ask you this. Do you eat food that's different from the Gentiles?"

"Well, no."

"Do you speak a different language at home?"

"No."

"Do you not feel comfortable in general social setting?"

"I do feel more comfortable here than when I'm in Israel."

"You are a typical western Diaspora Jew. You are culturally western. Not Jewish. You holding to a mirage that there is a Jewish culture for non-religious Jews is the product of brainwashing. That kind of thinking unnecessarily identifies Jews as targets. Jews like you and me should blend in and enjoy what we already enjoy without creating problems for ourselves."

"But we are Jewish."

"So what? People around us have Irish background or Scottish heritage or Scandinavian or German ethnicity. But they all assimilate. Why not the Jews? Why should we purposely make ourselves into targets unnecessarily?"

"But it is important to preserve Jewish existence."

"Why? I think it's more important to exist as human beings. Who cares if my descendants completely forget that they are Jewish. They will survive and thrive. They will live as members of the human race. That is the ideal."

"But Jewish people were almost annihilated in the holocaust and assimilation will finish Hitler's job."

"What are you? Hillel House pamphlet? A Chabad tract? If you are religious, you are religious. But if you are secular as I am, then who cares about the survival of an ancient, misogynous religion like Judaism? I am secular and an atheist. So are you. We can thrive being assimilated. All this talk of Jews being obligated to maintain their distinctive Jewish identity sounds more racist than anything I've read."

"But we've been victims and must stick together to survive."

"That's a bunch of BS. Jews who are secular should assimilate and even actively throw away their Jewish distinctions. We can survive and thrive as humans. That's what's important to me. To be a good human being."

The Flag

The whiteness of the wall was covered in red, white, and blue. The gigantic American flag seemed quite out of place so far away from America. But Robert seemed to feel at home gazing up at it in admiration.

"Why did you bring that big American flag here?" David asked, trying to hide the contempt in his voice.

"You should be happy to see the flag," Robert replied, clearly offended. "You are an American after all."

"I am a Jew, and I am in the Jewish state. The last thing I want to see is some Gentile symbol." David did not back down.

"Well, I am going to keep this flag in my side of the room," Robert said authoritatively. "I won't complain about what offensive thing you might hang up on your side of the room. I would appreciate it if you wouldn't complain about what I hang up on my side of the room."

"Good way to start as roommates," David said, not being able to find a good comeback.

"You started it, bud," Robert said and walked out of the room.

David felt a bad taste in his mouth, like he had taken a bite out of a rotten piece of meat. He was glad to get away from New York. He lived in Brooklyn and had many Jewish friends and neighbors, but he felt that something was missing. He could not put his finger on it, but he assumed that it was because New York was not Jewish enough. He did not feel ownership of the city and felt that it was because the country was not Jewish. David was certain that if he were to live in the Jewish state, where Jews controlled the country, he would feel more at home. For a long time, he saved money and applied to every agency possible that would offer scholarships to study in Israel. After many rejection letters, David finally procured a place in a scholarship program sponsored by the local Jewish community center. The last thing he wanted to see was the flag of a country he did not feel an ounce of loyalty towards.

"Hey, David," Susan said cheerfully as she pushed open the door.

"Why don't you just walk right in!" David said, irritated.

"The door was open, and I saw you through the crack so I just dropped in," Susan replied defensively. "You are not in a good mood, are you?"

"Look there," David said, pointing to the American flag.

"What do you want from me? To recite the pledge of allegiance to the flag?" Susan said sarcastically.

"I see that you share my sentiments," David said.

"What sentiment is that?" Susan said, curious.

"I don't like the fact that Robert has that flag up there," David explained.

"What's wrong with it?" Susan asked.

"I am in the Jewish state, for God's sake!" David exclaimed.

"Okay, okay. Don't have a cow," Susan said dismissively. "It's not like it's a Syrian flag."

"Yeah, but I came to get away from all that," David said loudly.

"America is the most pro-Jewish country in the world," Susan replied.

"Yeah, yeah, yeah," David waved off her comments. "That's what my parents always say. But I think they are being naïve."

"So, you think America is anti-semitic?" Susan said, teasing David.

"They are all against us," David said in anger.

"You should cool down, David," Susan said. "What's wrong?"

"Nothing!" David said, agitated.

"Let me guess," Susan took relish in playing the psychologist. "You had a fight with Robert over the flag."

"I don't think it takes a genius to figure that out," David replied contemptuously.

"Don't be that way," Susan said, clearly offended. "I'm going to come back when you are feeling better."

David felt a bit bad since Susan was a nice person whom he liked the most from the group of American exchange students at the university. What he liked most about her was that she seemed most in-tune with her Jewish identity. Unlike Robert, she saw herself first and foremost as a Jew and then secondly as an American. David could not understand how any Jew could feel himself American first and Jew second.

Susan was more surprised by David's reaction than she led on. Although she had not known David for a long time, she pictured him as a quiet, pensive type with a gentle disposition. But the recent outburst showed her that he had a temper. This intrigued her. She was curious to learn what the argument was about so she went to the student café attached to the dormitory building in the hope of spotting Robert. She wasn't disappointed.

"Robert, hi!" Susan said.

"Hi," Robert said, forcing a smile.

"Can I sit down?" Susan asked, assuming that Robert was ready to spill the beans.

"Sure," Robert said.

"I just saw David," Susan replied.

"Oh," Robert replied, trying to seem indifferent.

"He seemed upset," Susan said and received no response.

Susan continued, "Did you guys have a fight?"

"Yeah, you could say that," Robert said, feeling he needed to talk to someone.

"About the flag?" Susan said, nodding.

"Yeah," Robert gave himself up.

"Why did you bring that big flag with you?" Susan asked. "Just out of curiosity."

Robert looked at her face for a while, trying to see if she was being hostile. He concluded that Susan was genuinely interested. "I am loyal to America. I feel that it's been good to me, and I feel proud to be an American."

"Yeah," Susan said. "But do you have that flag in your room in the USA?"

"No," Robert said, looking down at the table. He knew what the next question was going to be.

"So, why here?" Susan did not disappoint.

"Okay," Robert said. "I will tell you. I feel myself American, and I believe that all American Jews should feel the same way. If they are more loyal to the State of Israel, then they should move here. After all, all Jews can automatically become Israelis if they want to. If Jews are willing to stay in America and choose America over Israel, then they should be more loyal to America."

"But there is anti-semitism in the USA," Susan said.

"You don't think everyone experiences some type of prejudice?" Robert said. "Italian immigrants had a difficult time because of prejudice against Italians. Particularly, Sicilians with dark skin suffered discrimination. But you don't see them bitching all the time about anti-semitism."

"Anti-semitism is only against Jews," Susan protested.

"Precisely," Robert commented. "We even invented a word to celebrate our otherness."

"Celebrate?" Susan demanded.

"Yes, celebrate," Robert responded. "It is like a badge of honor we wear as Jews. Other immigrants try to forget the bad and celebrate the good. We Jews on the other hand ignore our achievements and celebrate the bad experiences."

"Isn't that a bit harsh?" Susan asked. "You are a Jew. You should understand about the dangers of anti-semitism."

"Sure," Robert replied. "But I think that our fixation with anti-Semitism makes us more vulnerable. It's a ghetto mentality that castrates our pride and diminishes our achievements."

"So, should we encourage anti-semitism?"

"I am not saying that," Robert said quickly. "What I am saying is that we should not make ourselves into objects of hatred."

"What do you mean?" Susan asked, genuinely confused.

"First of all, consider this," Robert paused for effect. "If a person goes around saying, 'No one likes me,' then what would you think about him? You would think him a complete loser. Even if you liked him, you may ask yourself why others don't like him. The very fact that the comment came out of his mouth will cause you to re-evaluate your opinion of him. Most likely, the idea that others don't like him – an idea which he himself encourages – will cause you to develop contempt for him, which you would not otherwise have had. The same is true for a people. If we Jews keep going around saying that nobody likes us, then we ourselves are encouraging contempt from those who might be neutral or even favorably inclined toward us as a group or as individuals."

"I don't think that you are making any sense," Susan criticized.

"Look at the history," Robert said. "Why is it that everywhere Jews go, we are hated?"

"Anti-semitism," Susan concluded.

"Look, Susan, we are talking about people of different backgrounds, histories, languages, and cultures. It's not like they have made a collective pact to hate the Jews."

"Now, you are being sarcastic," Susan said.

"Sorry," Robert apologized. "But do you see my point? We Jews have to understand why there is recurring hatred against us wherever we are. Why doesn't this happen with other ethnic groups?"

Susan looked at Robert with anger in her eyes but could not offer any response.

"See, anti-semitism doesn't help explain it," Robert said. "It's just an epithet that makes us forget about the solution."

"I am not convinced," Susan said. "Do you have better reasons?"

"Okay," Robert replied. "I can come up with another good reason."

"Shoot," Susan said sarcastically.

Ignoring her clear sarcasm, Robert continued, "Let's suppose that you are playing football for Boston College and you say that you are more loyal to USC. Do you think that your teammates will appreciate your loyalty to your team's enemy?"

"I see where you are going with this," Susan said. "But I think America and Israel are different. We are allies."

"Do you know that there is a Jewish captain in the American Navy currently in prison in the USA for giving American military secrets to Israel?"

"Really?"

"Yeah," Robert said. "Israel and the USA are not such good friends as many would like to believe."

"Oh," Susan said, surprised.

"The American government and its security forces, like Homeland Security, will fundamentally question the status of a Jew who is more loyal to Israel than the USA. If shit hits the fan, will this Jew bat for America or for Israel? More power and influence a Jew has, this will become an increasingly important question for American security agencies."

"Interesting point," Susan disrupted.

"Please let me continue," Robert said. When Susan gave an apologetic nod, Robert continued, "Think about the American masses. They are suspicious of political loyalty to anything that's not American. Particularly, highly organized groups being loyal to non-American governments raises bright, red flags. It probably was the case in the popular psyche before September 11th. For instance, there was the McCarthy era right after World War II. But post-September 11th, it is so much more the case. So, when a bunch of Jews keep signaling to 300 million Americans that they are loyal to Israel, they are basically exclaiming, 'Shoot me, shoot me!'"

"I don't think that it's that extreme," Susan protested.

"They might not shoot you, right away, but it'll have negative consequences for the Jewish communities in the USA. Next thing you know, the FBI will be assassinating Jewish Senators for national security," Robert said in a serious tone.

"That won't happen," Susan objected.

"Yes, it won't if I can help it," Robert said. "If Jews in America are more loyal to America than Israel, and there is no doubt in the minds of those in government and among the masses, then Jews will be secure. But if there is doubt, I don't think we will be. The way Jews like David carry on, I would even be suspicious of Jews, if I were a non-Jew in America."

"There are more Jews like David than there are Jews like you, Robert," Susan said.

"Then, we are in trouble," Robert said. "No wonder Jews keep suffering pogroms and genocides. The pattern repeats. You know that the ancient Romans doubted Jewish loyalty to the Roman Empire? It was because they could not trust even Roman citizens among Jews that they destroyed Israel and took away any possibility for Jews to advance in the Roman Empire."

"You sure about your facts?" Susan asked, suspicious.

"Do your research and prove me wrong, Susan. I doubt that you can," Robert replied.

"I dunno," Susan said, shaking her head.

"I am positive about my position," Robert said. "So, I guess you could say that I am trying to dispel the stereotype that Jews are more loyal to Israel than their home country of America. Also, I am trying to get Jews who are citizens of the USA to realize the danger they are putting all Jews into by being super Jews loyal to Israel."

"I see," Susan said pensively.

"Sorry, Susan, but I have to go to class," Robert said, standing up.

"See you later," Susan waved goodbye as Robert left.

Robert sat there and watched Susan leave. He was feeling a bit embarrassed that he had become too excited in the course of the conversation. He was beginning to regret coming to Israel. Although he knew that he would run into problems trying to enlighten others about his point of view, he had not really known how that would feel. Furthermore, he felt that he was beginning to develop a kind of reputation and that made him feel uncomfortable. But Robert was convinced that this had to be done. He felt certain that the future survival of the Jewish community depended on him. Feeling reinvigorated by his sense of duty and commitment to the Jewish people, he marched out of the café and towards the library. He was going to read about pogroms to come up with more evidence for his claims.

"Hey, Robert!" Robert heard someone yell. "Hey, Robert, wait up!"

"What is it?" Robert asked as he turned around to identify the screamer. "It's you, Marc!"

"Yeah, it's me," Marc said. "And I have terrible news!"

Robert stared at Marc's disheveled curly hair. It looked as if he hasn't washed it for days. It gave Marc a wild appearance that matched the crazy look in his eyes which didn't seem capable of focusing on Robert's face. Robert felt concern come over him.

"It's horrible," Marc said. "So terrible!"

"What happened?" Robert said, feeling his apprehension give way to Marc's cranky voice.

"He was killed!"

"Who was killed?"

"Him!" Marc said. "The famous Senator!"

"Who?" Robert begged for the answer.

"Senator Daniel Baumberger!" Marc yelled, distraught.

"Senator Baumberger?" Robert asked. "How did that happen?"

"He was campaigning for the Presidency in the state of California and a group of young men came and shot him."

"Why would anybody do that?" Robert asked, puzzled.

"No one really knows what the cause was," Marc said.

"But he was a very popular Senator," Robert said. "I don't understand."

"Let's go to a room with a TV," Marc said. "I bet we can find answers there."

"Okay," Robert said and followed Marc, who seemed to have forgotten that Robert was accompanying him and rushed ahead.

"Can we come in?" Marc said as Robert finally stood next to him.

"Sure thing," Rachel said and practically rushed Robert and Marc into her room.

"What's going on?" Marc practically yelled.

"Shut up!" Someone yelled from a crowded room full of people.

"Sorry about that," Marc uttered as he sat down on the floor. Robert stood by the door and watched the TV intensely.

"We don't know why the popular Senator was shot. It came as a surprise to everyone," a journalist at the scene of the crime said on TV.

"Can you tell us if anyone heard anything said as the Senator was being shot?" a news anchor with a serious look asked from the newsroom.

"Yes, I have an eyewitness here who said he heard something," the journalist said. Turning to the eyewitness, the journalist asked, "You said you heard something that gunmen said as they shot the Senator. Could you tell us what was said?"

"Yes, of course," the witness said, looking a bit embarrassed. The look on journalist's face showed she was puzzled by the witness's expression.

"Well," the witness hesitated.

"Yes?" the journalist prodded unprofessionally.

"One of the gunmen yelled that the Senator's pro-Israel push in the Congress was responsible for the latest rise in terrorism."

"You can't be serious!" the journalist said. It was clear that she was taking the comment personally.

"Hey, lady, I am just telling you what he said," the witness said defensively. It was clear he was not happy to relay the message.

"Yes, I understand," the journalist tried to compose herself. "Did you hear anything else?"

"Another gunman said that if we don't stop the Jews, America will be terrorized," the witness said.

"Were the gunmen Arabs?" the news anchor blurted out.

"No, they are not," the journalist said, clearly still in shock. "They were four white Caucasian males from northern California."

"Were they Muslims?" the news anchor prodded in disbelief.

"No," the journalist said. "Nothing indicates that they are Muslim."

"They are not Muslim!" the witness interrupted. "They are good o' American boys with a heavy northern Californian accent. They probably have never been outside California in their life."

The journalist gawked at the witness like he had shot the Senator. The news anchor gawked at the TV screen as if he wanted to punish the witness through his TV monitor.

The news anchor composed himself and said, "So, we can rule out terrorism as a possibility."

"Can you believe the nerve?" Marc exclaimed.

"It's anti-semitism!" Rachel said. "A bunch of rednecks from California who hate Jews shot the Jewish Senator."

"It's horrible!" Robert said. "But I don't think it was just a general hatred against Jews."

"Oh, shut up!" someone exclaimed from the back of the room.

"Sit down, asshole!" some angry voice which Robert did not recognize yelled.

"Hey!" Robert yelled back. "I am Jewish myself and I hate what happened."

The room became silent except for the sounds coming out of the TV.

"But I have to say that it wasn't pure anti-semitism that's at fault," Robert said.

"Let's hear him out," Rachel said, sensing a renewed irritation in the room.

"You see," Robert said. "Americans are very edgy right now. September 11th triggered terror, and Americans no longer feel safe at home. All the security measures, such as planes being grounded, might be needed to ensure safety, but they are making Americans more and more uneasy. They feel that they do not have control over their own destiny. Then, last week happened. When the Empire State Building was blown up by heavy explosives at the base beams, it was the last straw. Americans are furious beyond control. But they no longer have a target, like Sadam Hussein. And where are they going to ferret out the terrorists who did this? There are no targets."

"So, just blame the Jews," Marc said, giving Robert a look that could kill. "Is that what you are saying?"

"No, I am not saying that they have the right to kill the Jews or even blame the Jews," Robert said defensively. "All I am saying is that many people are looking for people to blame."

"But why us Jews?" Rachel said.

"Because we are always defending Israel," Robert said.

"But America is pro-Israel!" Marc said.

"No," Robert said. "America has no loyalty to Israel or to Jews. Israel was useful during the Cold War, and Jews were good for providing campaign funds. No one actually felt loyalty to us for non-utilitarian purposes."

"It's bullshit!" someone yelled.

"No, it's not," Robert said. "Jews have visibly supported Israel and that raised red flags in the minds of many Americans who were suspicious of the situation in the Middle East. The US President wanted the roadmap for peace to go forward. When the Israeli Prime Minister objected and Jewish Senators in the USA supported him, that raised red flags among Americans even more."

"Yeah, but Senator Baumberger was popular," Rachel said.

"In the past, yes," Robert said. "Perhaps before September 11th, he had a chance to become the President. But not now."

"He has a point in that regard," Marc relented. "Senator Baumberger was recently in or near the last place. He did not make any screw-ups, so it's a surprise that he was losing so horribly in the primaries."

"Yes, that's right," Robert said. "It's because Senator Baumberger was loyal to Israel that he was so unpopular with American Democrats. Both Democrats and Republicans were traumatized by recent events, and they do not want anybody in power showing undue loyalty to foreign powers."

"But the USA and Israel are allies," Rachel said with a faint voice.

"Yes," Robert said, trying to suppress his irritation. "I hear that comment all the time. But let's face it. It's a new world we live in. The process of change started on September 11th, and it has not stopped."

"I hate to admit it, but Robert may have a point," Marc said.

"I was dreading this moment, and that's why I came to Israel. I wanted to raise the importance of Jewish loyalty to the country of their citizenship. I was particularly concerned for American Jews who tended to put the Israel issue to the foreground of political discussions. I feared that we Jews were shooting ourselves on the foot by drawing attention to ourselves in ways that would undo our community."

"But this is an isolated incident," Rachel objected.

"I don't think so," Robert said. "You watch and see. This is the beginning of the end of the American Jewish community. If I were you, I would move to Australia."

"You go to Australia," someone yelled. "I was born in New York, and I will die in New York."

"You may get your wish," Robert said.

"Get the fuck out!" someone yelled.

"Yeah," couple more people joined in. "Fuck off!"

"I'm leaving," Robert said. "But Jews should have been more loyal to the USA than Israel. Now, we'll pay for our allegiance to Israel."

The Weakling

He gazed up at the face of Jesus Christ, tied to a post, contorted pain frozen for timelessness. He marveled at how the beautiful creation of art could capture such agony. It seemed to him to be a cosmic contrast: beauty with ugliness, the good with the bad, glory with humiliation. The suffering of the Savior immortalized, so that visitors, such as he, could come and stare at the paradoxical form.

What could have moved the artistic genius to create something so powerful? Antoni Gaudi was a devout Catholic Christian who credited his God Jesus Christ with his artistic inspiration. Gaudi gave credit to his God for creating him and for imbuing him with artistic talents. Gaudi gave honor to God whenever he could and conscientiously tried to make others know that the glory for his work should belong to Christ Jesus. How could such a believer portray Jesus in such a humiliated state? There Jesus was, tied to a post in helplessness, his face testifying to the suffering he endured. How could a follower of Christ exult such a suffering?

David pondered such thoughts as he bore a hole in Jesus' face with his intense glare. It seemed to him that a savior should be powerful. It seemed odd that anyone could worship someone who was so weak and helpless. He felt that he would rather be the Pharisees who were able to put Jesus to the cross.

David was entering a world of business. There were sharks out there. There were Pharisees and Sadducees, all around. They had power. They had influence. They could make your future or break your future. They could get you black-listed so that you wouldn't be able to get a job in the business world ever again. They could put you to the cross. He preferred to side with the Pharisees and the Sadducees; not with this weakling Jesus who was tied to a post, awaiting his execution, his death.

"I can't understand why anyone would honor such a weakling," David blurted out loud, defying the intense feeling of reverence that the powerful art work was creating inside his heart.

"You are talking about the statue?" a young Spanish girl with a gentle face asked without giving away even a bit of surprise.

David's pale white face turned bright red, and he froze. The beautiful Latina's peaceful face broke its mysterious peace with a flood of laughter. There, the two stood in front of the statue, one in utter misery and the other in a strange exaltation.

"Yes," David said, trying to compose himself. But he felt embarrassed like the way he felt in front of the girl he was infatuated with when his best friend let her know that he liked her. That was 15 years ago. He vowed never to be that embarrassed again and succeeded in keeping his vow until that moment.

"I am sorry," the Latina with a heavenly smile said to David. Her apology made it worse. David felt like a little kid in front of a domineering Kindergarten teacher in control, who made him wash his mouth out with soap after mistaking him for his best friend who uttered the F-word and then apologized after his guilt-ridden best friend confessed.

David tried not to look into her eyes for fear of giving himself away. "That's okay," David said, trying to sound unaffected as much as possible.

"My name is Susana," the smiling Latina said.

"My name is David," David said, not extending his hand for a handshake because it was drenched with guilt sweat.

"I am a student at the Universidad Complutense de Madrid," Susana said softly, trying to make up for her uproarious laughter.

"I am a student at Haverford College," David replied.

"Where is that?" Susana asked bluntly.

"In Philadelphia," David replied. "Well, not exactly in Philadelphia, but in a nearby suburb."

"What's a suburb?" Susana asked.

David looked at the expressionless, but warm, face that was before him. It never occurred to him that he would ever have to explain what a suburb is to anyone. But then, it was the first time ever that he left the American soil.

"A suburb is a residential area near a city," David replied, feeling self-satisfied that he was able to come up with an adequate definition in such a short time and after a humiliating episode. He knew he was destined for success. All he had to do was to try his best to maintain control at all times.

"Oh, I see," Susana said and smiled. "Are you a tourist here?"

"Yes, I am," David answered. "In fact, it's the first time that I am out of my country."

"You are kidding!" Susana said in utter surprise.

Susana's surprise transferred the demon of laughter to David. David could not stop laughing. He felt a bit guilty as Susana looked down at the floor. It reminded him of the sadness of a class-mate in kindergarten whose dress was dirtied with dirt and worms by his mischievous best friend. He stood there and did nothing because he was afraid that his best friend would consider him a wimp.

"I am sorry," David said. "It's just that you looked so surprised."

David knew that he made a mistake as soon as the words left him. Susana did not say anything.

"It's just that I never met anyone who did not know what a suburb is," David tried to explain himself. That made it worse.

"So, you are laughing at my stupidity," Susana said without mincing words.

"No, it's not that at all," David replied. "I guess you caught me off guard."

Susana did not respond. David could not stand the silence. He hated it when his girlfriend gave him the silent treatment every time she felt that he did something wrong. In fact, if he had to point to one thing for breaking up with his girlfriend of one year, it was the silent treatments, which seemed to intensify with each advancing day. He was either making more mistakes or she was growing more irritable. Either way, he did not like the way it made him feel. He felt helpless. So, he broke up with her.

"Can I make it up to you?" David proposed. Susana looked up at him.

"May I take you to coffee?" David felt better because he was regaining control of the situation.

Susana looked at him and held out for a second or two. "Okay."

"Great!" David said, producing a smile that he had practiced for weeks for his job interviews.

They walked away from Sagrada Familia. David did not even give a second glance to the suffering statue.

They walked and walked, but were not able to spot a café.

"We must have made a wrong turn," David tried his hand at levity, as he assumed that Susana was growing restless. "I'm sure one café will turn up, soon."

Susana looked at David and smiled. "Don't worry, David. It's a nice day, and we are both on vacation."

That broke the ice for further conversation.

"So, you are on vacation, too?" David asked.

"Yes, it's our Easter vacation," Susana replied.

"What do you study at the university?" David asked.

"I study psychology," Susana replied.

"You are not going to psychoanalyze me, are you?" David tried to joke.

"Of course, not," Susana said. "I'm on vacation from psychology."

"Uh, oh," David commented. "That doesn't sound good. Did you do horribly on your exams?"

"Hardly," Susana replied, looking a bit offended. "I had the best grades in my class. After being submerged in the world of psychology, it's nice to take a vacation from it."

"So you are on an artistic tour of Barcelona?" David asked.

"Well, that and more," Susana said. David wondered what other things she had in mind. "David, here's a café."

"Oh, good," David reacted. "Let's go in."

David and Susana sat down and ordered coffee.

"What have you seen so far?" David asked.

"Basically, just the Sagrada Familia," Susan answered. "I just arrived."

"Me, too," David said, excited.

"Good, " Susan said. "Then, we can see the city, together."

David was taken aback by her forthright manner. This girl did not know if he came with anyone. She did not know who he really was. How could she just trust him like that. Her spontaneity impressed David as rash and lacking self-control.

"Okay," David said. Her impulsiveness was his advantage. He was afraid that this trip would turn out to be a boring, impersonal trip. Now, he did not need to fear any more. It was clear that Susana was a fun person. And he felt comfortable around her. But most importantly, Susana was absolutely beautiful.

"Are you vacationing alone?" David asked because he wanted to know what he was getting himself into.

"Yes," Susana replied.

"You came all the way to Barcelona on your own?" David asked. "You have relatives here?"

"All these questions," Susana said and smiled.

David felt awkward. "How else will I get to know you?"

"You are right," Susana said still smiling. "I have no relatives or friends in Barcelona. And that is the reason I am here. I want to get to know a place which I don't know at all."

"It's a part of Spain, right?" David said jokingly, although not intentionally trying to offend Susana.

"Barcelona prides itself in its Catalan culture, which has some distinctive qualities not found in Madrid," Susan responded graciously. "Take for instance, the works of Gaudi. You won't find anything like that in Madrid."

"Really?"

"Not to my knowledge," Susana said, taking David's comment literally as a question.

"Oh, I meant," David tried to explain what he meant with the last question-sounding response. On second thought, David decided that it would be simpler not to open up a new can of worms, so after a second's pause, he said, "That's surprising given that Gaudi is such an important artist."

"So, you know about Gaudi?" Susana said. "I am impressed."

"Oh, stop it. You are embarrassing me," David said. Susana looked puzzled. "I just read the little section on *Let's Go Spain*."

"Let's go Spain?" Susana asked, puzzled.

"Oh," David said, realizing that he was talking to someone from a completely different culture. "It's a guidebook that American students use the most."

"I see," Susana said and smiled.

"And having been to the church, I could see why he was influential," David said. "His art is very powerful."

"It's beautiful," Susana agreed. "I love his works. They invoke peace."

"You know," David responded. "Come to think about it, I understand what you mean."

"How about you?" Susana said. "Did you come alone?"

"Yes, I did," David answered, relieved that she was now asking the questions.

"What about your friends?"

"I had this girlfriend in college, and we were planning to come together," David answered. "But we broke up just before spring break."

"I am sorry to hear that," Susana said.

"No, it's okay," David said. "Really, I am okay. Besides, I broke up with her." David felt a little vulnerable. "It was for the best."

Susana gave a look of sympathy. David did not like it.

"She traded her ticket for a ticket to Cancun, the party place for American college students during spring break."

Susana did not relent. The look of pity made David feel he had to prove himself.

"No love lost. It was for the best," David said. "And now, I am in this beautiful city, admiring Gaudi's glorious art."

"Good for you," Susana said. David felt better.

"Although I have to confess that the last statue was a bit troubling," David said.

"In what way?"

"I don't know," David said. "It was just troubling. Like there was a type of innate, implicit dualism."

Susana looked as if she was trying to understand what he was saying. It reminded David of his days in kindergarten when he tried to convince his mom why Transformers were the greatest invention of all time.

"It seems odd how Gaudi uses his soft, rounded, non-violent technique to portray intense suffering, that's all."

Susana nodded and said, "I see. It's pure genius how Gaudi captures the suffering on Christ's face. I have never seen anything quite like it."

Susana did not understand what David meant, but David knew the blame was his. He did not tell Susana what he really thought – what he was thinking when she approached him – because he did not want Susana to think ill of him. David looked at the empty coffee cups.

"Shall we go and explore the city further?" David said, trying to change the subject.

"Okay," Susana said, upbeat.

They both agreed that the Gaudi House in the center of town should be the next stop. Since they both had a ticket for the open-top tourist bus that allowed them unlimited rides on the tourist bus for major tourist sites, they decided to take this mode of transportation. It meant that they had to retrace their steps to Gaudi's church. David felt a little uneasy about it as the place held his first dark secret in Barcelona. He only met Susana, but he was already hiding his thoughts and feelings from her. He remembered that his ex-girl friend always accused him of being dishonest with his feelings. He felt a bit pained in his stomach.

The tourist bus came soon enough. It made David feel that the expensive ticket was worth the price. He felt he needed fresh air to slap him around a bit. Then, it struck him that there had been a long period of silence. David worried that Susana was giving him the silent treatment. She must have suspected him of being dishonest with his feelings.

"I love this tourist bus," David said to Susana, trying to sound cheerful. It was really the only safe subject that David could think of as Sagrada Familia occupied the landscape before them.

"It is nice," Susana said without showing any malice.

David felt suspicious. Was she hiding something? Was her peaceful expression a cover for her pity? Was she thinking about his breaking up with his girlfriend?

"So, do you have a boyfriend?" David ask Susana.

"No," Susana said and looked more closely at him.

David felt that she was looking for something, but he had no idea what.

"Too busy with work?" David asked.

Susana looked disappointed. David did not know why.

"I don't really work, since I am focusing on my studies," Susana said.

"Yeah, I meant study," David said. "In America, we use the term 'work' for 'study'."

Susana looked at David with her big, brown eyes, which glittered under the sun.

"And I guess that makes complete sense," David said. "After all, that's what we do. We students, I mean. We study, and that's our work."

"I agree," Susana said.

"I mean, it's intense," David said. "Study can be very intense, more intense than work. I am actually glad that I am graduating and going to full-time work in a few months. No more sleepless nights, studying. It will be eight to five. And I will be able to leave work at work and just have fun at home."

"That's great," Susana said.

"Aren't you curious what kind of work I am going to do?" David said, a little hurt that Susana was not showing more interest in his life.

"I am," Susana said succinctly.

"Okay, I will tell ya," David said. "I will be working for an investment bank. The pay is good, and it will be in New York. What more can a guy ask for, right?"

Susana smiled.

"I am quite excited to be going to the Big Apple," David said. Susana looked at David as if she were not convinced.

"I really am," David said as if he could force her to be convinced by repeating his words. "I am excited because if you could make it in New York, you can make it anywhere, right? And I am ready to take a big bite out of the Big Apple. Four years of Haverford trained me for success."

Susana's beautiful brown eyes seemed to get bigger. David remembered the girl he liked in kindergarten. He hid a big Hershey's chocolate bar inside her desk. When she discovered the chocolate, with a little note from a secret admirer, her brown eyes grew bigger and bigger. It was the first time that David observed such a reaction by someone's eyes.

"Yes-sir-ee!" David said for dramatic effect. "I am going to be big. No, bigger than big."

Susana smiled.

"Oh, we are already here," David said.

David and Susana took a guided tour of Gaudi's house. There was not much art by Gaudi in the house. Susana seemed a bit disappointed. David was less upset as he enjoyed accounts of Gaudi's life. Four years of being a history major fostered David's interest in important figures in history. David wondered what made people great. And as he was convinced in the One Man theory that one great man can make great things happen in history, he tried to understand personal and social ingredients behind powerful people of history. David listened intently for clues. What made Gaudi what he was? How did Gaudi obtain influence as an artist?

Susana looked over at David with a look of boredom more than once during the tour. David smiled each time. He wondered if the fact that the tour was in English had anything to do with it. David felt guilty again since because of him, she was taking an English tour. But David dispelled all remorse when he realized that her English was good, although she missed some colloquialisms now and then.

The guided tour ended up on the roof of the house. Susana looked relieved. When she saw the works of Gaudi on the roof, she seemed to be rejuvenated.

The Whistle

"Do you know what I hear?" Faisal said.

"A whistle?" I asked, genuinely puzzled by the anger in his voice.

"No," Faisal said, dismissively. "I hear a 'Fuck You!'"

"Faisal, you can't be serious!" I said, alarmed.

"Actually, it's worse than 'Fuck You!'" Faisal said. "It's a combination of 'Fuck You', 'Bloody Bastard', 'Asshole', and 'Your Mother" all rolled into one."

"Isn't that a bit extreme?" I asked rhetorically. I could not believe my ears!

"I consider it more offensive than the strongest racist epithet thrown at me by a religious Jew," Faisal said. "That's how seriously I see it."

"But, it's just a whistle," I said.

"For you, it may be just a whistle," Faisal said. "But for me it is a targeted and intentional harassment of the most horrible kind."

"How can you say that!" I said, not being able to believe my ears.

"It is a way I am dehumanized and my personal dignity stripped away."

"I can't see how you could say that," I said, trying to show him how ridiculous he sounded. "How could a whistle be worse than calling you a goddamn fuckin' Arab?"

"Hey!" Faisal said.

"See!" I said triumphantly. "You are upset!"

"You seemed like you were enjoying that a little too much," Faisal said. "Even though you are my best friend, you are not Arab, you know."

"So, you are saying that if an Arab called you a goddamn fuckin' Arab, it would be okay," I said, somewhat irritated.

"I have to be totally honest with you, Zacky," Faisal said. "If an Arab calls me that, I would certainly not mind it as much as others saying it."

I glared at him and was lost for words.

"Zacky, sorry, man. You are thinking that I am picking on Jews."

"No, not at all!" I lied.

"It would not matter to me if the person were Jewish or non-Jewish," Faisal explained. "If he were not of the Arab race then it would be very offensive."

"I guess I could see that," I relented. "In-group, out-group thing."

"Yeah, I guess something like that," Faisal nodded. "Just consider this. You know in rap music, blacks call each other 'Nigga'?"

"Yeah, I have heard that," I said.

"It's not just in music," Faisal said. "When I was in America for an internship at the United Nations, I lived in a predominantly black neighborhood in New York. There, I heard blacks…."

"You mean, African Americans?" I interrupted him. "That's the politically correct term, you know."

"I know," Faisal said. "The reason I use the term black is because not everyone living there were African Americans. There were Africans studying at Columbia University, who wanted to go back to South Africa to help build it with their newly gained education. There were Jamaicans, who preferred to be called Jamaicans, rather than African Americans. And there were blacks from South America who preferred to see themselves as Latino. Now, there is diversity in the black community, and many black communities actually like to celebrate the diversity. It makes the black people more complex and takes away the stereotype of 'simple black folk' in the American psyche. Besides, I am using the term 'black' in the spirit of 'Black is Beautiful!' movement."

"Okay," I said, feeling overwhelmed. "I see you have thought about the issue."

"Can I continue with what I was saying?" Faisal asked me.

"Sorry," I felt a little stupid. "Please do continue."

"The fact is that blacks sometimes call each other nigger," Faisal said. "Sometimes, it's in a derogatory way, but it's not always that way."

"What do you mean?" I asked.

"You are interrupting again," Faisal said in a sing-song voice.

"Okay," I said, feeling that I was making too many concessions.

"As I was saying, sometimes a black person calls another person a nigger to insult him. But other times, it could be in an endearing way. In other words, the same derogatory term can be used negatively or positively."

"It's like what my Korean friend told me," I seized a moment of silence to interject.

"What did he say?" Faisal looked interested.

"He said that in rural areas in Korea, a mother calls her son 'Shit-Dog'."

"You must be shitting me!" Faisal said, laughing at his own play on words.

I gave him a look of disapproval and continued, "Of course, they don't use the English word."

"What's it in Korean?"

"He told me," I said. "Let me see if I can remember."

"You gotta remember words like that," Faisal said, lightening up. "It could be useful."

"Oh, I remember now," I said. "It's something like 'Dong-gi'. No! It's 'Tong-gae'! Yeah, that's it! 'Tong-gae'."

"Tong-gae?" Faisal said. "It actually does not sound like a curse word at all. It has a gentle touch."

"I guess a Korean hearing it might say otherwise," I said.

"You have a point," Faisal said. "So, you are right. It's like that."

"I see," I said, nodding.

"And sometimes, it's just a way of addressing someone," Faisal said. "Like when you use the terms, 'dude' or 'brother'."

"No way!" I exclaimed.

Faisal looked at my seriousness and smiled. "Way!"

"You have spent way too much time in the USA," I said, being offended at his teasing me.

"Come on, Zacky," Faisal said laughing. "I'm just joking."

"Yeah, at my expense!"

"Sorry, dude," Faisal said. "But you see how a derogatory term that is totally taboo in a white community can be used in different in-group situations?"

"You are telling me basically that if I were black, I can get away with calling someone a nigger."

"I don't know about that," Faisal shook his head. "But certainly more so than if you said it as a white person."

"Okay," I admitted. "I see your point. The same term can be differently charged based on who utters it."

"The nature of the speaker gives a kind of value to the word. Words are innately neutral."

"But some words are innately charged," I protested.

"Like what?" Faisal asked.

"Okay," I said. "Since we are talking about racial slurs, I have one for you."

"Give it to me!" Faisal said.

"How about the word 'chink'?" I asked. "I guess it's like that with 'nigger', too, come to think about it."

"Since you brought up the word, 'chink', let's stick with that," Faisal said.

"Okay," I agreed. "It's a negatively charged word. You can't get away with calling an Asian person a chink and get away with it. It's a negatively charged word, whoever utters it."

"I don't know if 'chink' is a good example, actually," Faisal said. "But it's good for illustrating an important point."

"And that is?"

"You know how I said that a word is neutral but it is given a value by the speaker of that word?"

"Yeah?"

"That's not the only way a word is given a value," Faisal said. "A word can be given a value by its use."

"Please explain," I said, puzzled. "I don't see what you mean."

"Let me think," Faisal said, squinting his eyes to come up with a good explanation.

I always appreciated Faisal's intelligence. He had fresh ideas and made me think about mundane things from a different perspective. I wondered where he got all his ideas. I looked at him and examined his face to see if I could get a clue. His olive skin was without blemish and his proud Arab mustache was coming along nicely. Faisal told me a week ago that a mustache is a sign of masculinity in the Arab community. I thought about my Korean friend and how he could not grow a mustache and smiled.

"What's funny?" Faisal said, confused.

"No, it's nothing," I said. "I was just thinking about my Korean friend."

"Tong-gae!" he teased me.

"Yeah," I said, glad that I was let off easy.

"I think I found an explanation that will make sense," Faisal said. "The way a word is used gives a type of charge to the word."

"Okay," I said slowly, still confused.

"You know that 'chink' is a word, right?" Faisal said.

"Yes," I said.

"Where's that Oxford Dictionary?" Faisal asked.

"I believe you, dude," I said.

"No, this is important," Faisal said and walked off to get the dictionary.

I don't know how Faisal became such a perfectionist. It must be totally stressful to be so intense all the time. I was beginning to feel stressed just being in his presence. But I had to confess that I found the conversation interesting.

"I'm back," Faisal said. "Oxford English Dictionary defines 'chink' as 'a narrow opening or crack'. A second definition is 'a beam of light admitted by a chink.'"

"Okay," I said.

Faisal continued, "Oh, that's interesting!"

"What?" I asked in interest.

"It can also be used as a verb," Faisal said.

"Really?"

"Yeah," Faisal said. "As a verb, 'chink' means 'make a light, high-pitched ringing sound, as of glasses or coins striking together'."

"How interesting!" I said.

"You see," Faisal said. "The word is a legitimate English word. But at some point the word acquired a negative connotation. I bet it was because someone started calling an Asian person a 'chink'. Perhaps, it began as a playful comment without any malicious intent attached to it. You know how in comedies, they always show Chinese as having buckteeth?"

"Yeah," I said. "But that's nasty."

"Okay," Faisal relented. "It can be pretty derogatory."

"I bet someone of Chinese ethnicity would not appreciate that joke at all," I said.

"You are right," Faisal said. "But my point is that someone might have used the word, 'chink', first in a harmless way."

"Well...," I protested.

"At least, it did not have the offensive meaning it has today," Faisal said defensively. "I mean when it was first used."

"Okay," I said. "I could see that."

"It was just a word in the English language," Faisal said. "But as it became used by one person, two people, ten people, thousand people, and so on, to refer derogatorily to Asians, it became a racial slur."

"I now see what you mean when you say usage gives value to a word."

"Yes," Faisal nodded. "Usage is one of the ways a word is given a value, either positive or negative. In the case of 'chink', negative. And you know what?"

"What?"

"The usage becomes so frequent that it becomes general knowledge what that usage is," Faisal said.

"You mean, people come to see that using the word 'chink' to refer to an Asian person is racist?" I commented.

"Precisely," Faisal said. "And looky here! The Oxford English Dictionary includes the racial slur."

"Really?" I asked, surprised.

"Yes, my friend," Faisal said. "'Chink' is defined as 'a Chinese person'. And the dictionary notes that it is informal and offensive usage."

"That's funny. My Korean friend tells me that Koreans are called 'chinks' as well," I said.

"Well, Chinese people and Korans look very much alike," Faisal said.

"Yeah," I said. "It's like Indian people being called 'Paki' in England."

"What's a 'Paki'?"

"It's short for Pakistani, but it's used derogatorily in England against Pakistanis and Indians," I explained.

"That's interesting," Faisal said. "Let's look up 'Paki'."

"Let's not," I said.

"I am curious. If English people use the term, it should have a detailed explanation in the Oxford Dictionary, right?"

"Okay," I said, trying to humor him.

"Yes, it does have the entry," Faisal said. "The dictionary defines 'Paki' as 'a Pakistani' and notes that it is British informal usage and offensive."

"It actually identifies it explicitly as a British usage?" I asked, surprised.

"Yes," Faisal answered. "That must be why I never heard the term in the USA."

"That's enough with the dictionary," I said.

"Okay," Faisal said and stood up.

"Where are you going?" I asked.

"To put the dictionary back," Faisal said.

I let out a grunt but did not say anything. Faisal was such a perfectionist and always so fastidious, it irritated me. But he had other redeeming features, so I tried to focus on his good points.

"How did we get to looking up 'Paki' in the dictionary?" I asked, trying to remember the original discussion.

"I can't believe it," Faisal said. "You already forgot why this conversation started?"

"Sorry, bud," I said, genuinely apologetic.

"You thought I should not have been offended by someone whistling at me," Faisal said.

"Right," I said. "It seems harmless."

"Look," Faisal said, seriously. "It's not like playing in a basketball game and getting booed by the opposing side's fans."

"Say what?"

"What I am trying to say is that this is my life," Faisal said. "I live day in and day out and get harassed by people whistling at me."

"You must be kidding me," I said.

"Yes," Faisal said. "Whistling has taken on a value here through usage. When people whistle at me, it is meant in an offensive way."

"Maybe, they are trying to get your attention," I said, trying to reason with him.

"Do you like it when people whistle at you to get your attention?" Faisal asked with glaring eyes.

I pulled back a little in surprise. "I guess not."

"I am not a pet dog," Faisal said. "You whistle at a pet dog, not at human beings."

"I see your point," I said.

"It is dehumanizing, and it deprives me of my dignity as a human being."

"I see how you can be offended," I said, trying to appease him.

As if I unleashed a floodgate, Faisal said in a loud voice, "You see, it is offensive even if they are merely trying to get my attention because they are treating me like their pet dog. But I don't just get whistles from people who are trying to get my attention."

"What do you mean?"

"People whistle at me in an act of aggression," Faisal said.

"You have to explain yourself on this point," I said, trying to understand where he was coming from. "I am listening."

"If someone is pissed off at me for whatever reason, he would whistle at me. I might have actually offended him or it might be a misunderstanding, but he would whistle as an act of aggression to show his displeasure."

"Why would he whistle?"

"I will tell you why," Faisal replied. "We live in a politically correct culture. If he cursed at me or said something verbal, he might be afraid about consequences for his image. What would people around him say? But if he whistled, then he knows he is irritating me. And for him, it is a coded way to express his 'Fuck You'. And he can deceive himself that it's just a whistle. He is innately a good person because he didn't curse or say horrible things, while experiencing the satisfaction at making me feel bad."

"So you are saying what's inside him convicts him rather than what comes out of him?"

"It is true that his intentions convict him," Faisal answered. "He wants to say something unkind or horrible to me, so his intentions are bad.

But I want to stress the point that there is something uttered."

"A whistle?"

"Yes," Faisal said. "It is a verbal expression, just like the words 'chink' or 'nigger'."

"Yes, but," I tried to protest.

"Just like these words took on a negative value, a whistle can take on such a negative value through usage."

"But whistle is not a word," I protested.

"Do you know that some tribes communicate by whistling? Soldiers in combat sometimes communicate by whistling. Each sound or collection of sounds are given values so that the language of whistle could be understood," Faisal explained. "Besides, what's a language but a collection of sounds arranged in a certain way?"

"But how do you know that they are whistling at you?"

"Because they generally glare at you and whistle," Faisal said. "Also, they don't whistle a tune usually. It's just a series of cacophonous, aggressive whistle sounds."

"I see," I said. It was hard for me to see that a whistle was the same as calling an Asian a 'chink'.

"Also, they start whistling when they see me," Faisal said. "It's like in some racist areas, a policeman turns the siren in his police car on just when he drives by a black person just to intimidate him. Or to get a laugh at surprising him. It may be funny to these racist cops, but it's not funny to the black man just walking in the street."

"Yeah, I heard about profiling," I said.

"Yes, some cops think that the people of color should be put in their place by intimidation."

"But in regards to whistling, who whistles at you?" I asked out of curiosity.

"You know, I am the only Arab person in my department in the university," Faisal said.

"But there are Arabs in the university," I said, feeling personally offended for some reason.

"Yes, you are right," Faisal said. "There are Arabs in the university. But I am also right in pointing out that I am the only Arab in my department."

"True," I conceded.

"It started in my department with this one Jewish guy," Faisal said.

"But everyone in your department is Jewish," I protested.

"Yes, I know that we are in the Jewish state," Faisal said with bitterness showing in his voice. "So, we are agreed that he is Jewish."

"Okay," I said, reluctantly.

"Well, that's not really important, I guess," Faisal said. "He started to whistle at me because he did not like me. I did not know what was going on at first, but gradually I understood that he was, in fact, saying, 'Fuck You', when he whistled at me."

"So, what did you do?" I asked.

"I asked him to stop whistling," Faisal said.

"Then, he stopped?" I asked.

"Well, at first he did," Faisal said. "But then he would make whistle-like sounds and pretend that he did not do it. What's worse was that he went and told his friends that I was an asshole and that I didn't like it when people whistled at me. Since some of them do not like Arabs anyway, they had fun whistling at me to irritate me. I think some of his friends who may not be racist whistled out of curiosity to see how I would react. Maybe some of them whistled to defend him. Anyhow, every time I would see his friends, they would whistle at me and look at me."

"Man, that's not cool!" I said.

"What started out as one Jewish guy hating me and harassing me turned into a widespread, institutionalized harassment. Both racist Jews and even non-racist Jews got involved in the act. They all knew that I did not like it, and that seemed to egg them on more."

"Sorry, dud," I said.

"The whistle took on a value of harassment," Faisal said. "And people started jumping backwards and forwards trying to justify their harassment. They know all the while that I did not like what they did. They knew."

"That sounds horrible," I said, feeling for my friend's pain. "What are you going to do?"

"I want them to ask forgiveness from the god that they serve and stop harassing me," Faisal said. "But it won't happen."

"Why not?"

"Because if I did not tell that one guy not to whistle, his friends would not have started whistling at me out of malice or curiosity. Or to defend their friend. You see, they have taken a bite out of the fruit of the knowledge of good and evil and they can't stop sinning."

"How can I help?" I said, wanting to alleviate his suffering.

"I don't know," Faisal said. "It's like a snowball, getting bigger and bigger. And I fear that it is headed toward a tragic end."

"For you?" I said. "I hope not."

"Not only for me," Faisal said. "A society that loses its ethical obligation to human dignity the way it has here is bound to experience some sort of divine wrath, bad karma, whatever you call it. How will everyone be able to redeem themselves? And it's not possible for such a snowballing effect to stop. I only see a bleak end."

I did not know what to say, so I tried to comfort him. After a while I left to come back home. It was late after all. All the way home, I thought and thought. I felt terrible for Faisal. But I was more concerned that Faisal was so affected by this than his prophecy of doom. I also felt a little bit afraid that he might go insane. Honestly, some of the things that he said sounded crazy. Was there something I could do to help? Maybe if I could show him that someone who cares about him like myself whistles at him, then he will realize that it is not malicious. Maybe he'll get more used to it. People get over little things that bother them, don't they? People have bad memories like child abuse, but they come to deal with it and live with it, don't they? It's better to face your troubles and fears than to avoid it, isn't it? Maybe I'll look for an opportune, harmless time to whistle. I want to help my best friend somehow. That's all I want to do. He knows I care about him and he knows that my intention is pure. We have been friends for a long time. It would only improve the situation. I will help. I will help him by making him face the abuse.

Acknowledgement

I would like to thank my best friend Ed Moseng for reading some of the stories and encouraging me.

About the Author

H. C. Kim lives in Cambridge, United Kingdom, and is a very prolific writer. This is his second collection of short stories. Kim's first collection, *Romeo and Juliet in Jerusalem and Other Short Stories,* published in 2003, also deals with themes of Jewish identity and the peace process. Kim has lived in Jerusalem for over three years under the auspices of The Goldsmith Foundation, Raoul Wallenberg Scholarship, Lady Davis Fellowship, the Hebrew University of Jerusalem, and the State of Israel.

www.ingramcontent.com/pod-product-compliance
Lightning Source LLC
Chambersburg PA
CBHW030427310726
48979CB00009B/1651/J

* 9 7 8 0 9 7 2 3 8 6 4 7 0 *